Dark Vision

by

Susan Vaughan

The DARK Files, Book 4

Dark Vision

Cover Art by *Lisa Dawn MacDonald*

The Wild Rose Press, Inc.
PO Box 708
Adams Basin, NY 14410-0708
Visit us at www.thewildrosepress.com

Publishing History
First Edition, 2024
Trade Paperback ISBN 978-1-5092-5425-5
Digital ISBN 978-1-5092-5426-2
Previously Published 2018 by Gullwood Press

The DARK Files, Book 4
Published in the United States of America

Chapter One

THE SIGHT OF her slammed Matt Leoni in the chest.

When Nadia Parker climbed into the limousine, he slid from the backseat to the rear-facing one, just catching a whiff of flowers, like the lilacs his mom used to have in vases. He stretched out and crossed his ankles. He'd steeled himself for this first meeting, but with every muscle tensed, it was a hell of a hard job looking like he didn't give a crap.

The hip-clinging top and skinny pants she wore showcased her long curvy body. The rust color brought out the highlights in her dark-gold hair. Reminded him how her fire and beauty had sidetracked him five years ago.

As if he needed reminding.

She took the seat beside Princess Sarika. When she saw him, her high-boned cheeks paled and hurt flashed in her green eyes. Like on the day he'd arrested her father for treason.

Her hand trembled as she stowed her go cup—black, no sugar if he remembered—in the holder. A vigorous shake of her head flicked hair onto her cheeks and across her shoulders. Longer than he remembered. Touchable. Sexy.

She was fiddling with her collar pin, an autumn leaf, so his one-eyed once-over shook her. Or maybe the fidgeting was just her. A bright-eyed dynamo, she was never still. Once she learned the reason for his presence, she'd be more than rattled. He couldn't let their past distract him. A life hung in the balance. Probably more than one. He couldn't fail, not again.

"Nadia," Sarika began, "I believe you know Matt Leoni."

"Yes. We've… met." Nadia wouldn't meet his gaze. No surprise. Her father's downfall had been a shock. She resented Matt for his part in the case, thought the worst of him. "What is he doing *here*?" Her voice, honey over velvet with a trace of Virginia southern, ignited a slow burn inside him.

Her green gaze flickered to his eye patch, then away. Having his vision limited pissed him off, even if the damage was temporary. Even if it wasn't. He sure as hell wanted no pity. Not from Nadia. Not from anybody.

"I'm here at Her Highness's request." That should be enough. He'd rather not explain that the Domestic Antiterrorism Risk Corps, better known as DARK, had a deeper role in his mission. He schooled his features into a noncommittal expression, with eyes that gave away nothing. His G-Man face, she'd once called it.

He clicked the intercom on the panel beside him. "Take us north for a while."

"Yes, sir."

The Embassy of Modena's limo rolled away from Nadia's small Bethesda, Maryland, hotel and turned onto Massachusetts Avenue, where buildings reflected the October morning sun. Encased in well-upholstered silence and the aroma of fine leather, they tooled past banks and posh businesses and cross streets that led to ritzier neighborhoods in this D.C. suburb.

A few of Matt's missions, like the one Sarika was bound to mention, had dumped him in with the ritzy crowd, but he preferred blue jeans to black ties. And this sure wasn't his kind of neighborhood. Or his kind of ride. No, give him the rumble of a bike beneath his butt and the freedom of the open road.

Shaking off his thoughts, he checked the windows. Normal shopper and business traffic.

The princess had vouched for her long-time chauffeur's loyalty and sealed mouth, but the jockey-size guy couldn't be much protection. Matt would beef up security. Give old Stefan a vacation until the princess's safety was assured.

"Matt is here because I know I can trust him," Sarika said, her upper-class British accent infusing the statement with gravitas.

Nadia huffed. "Trust is relative."

Apparently ignoring the bitter tone, the princess continued, "Matt's unfortunate injury is the reason we are lucky to have his services. Stopping a terrorist plot in Belgium, a successful mission, was it not, Matt?"

Successful, but at too high a price. "That particular reign of terror ended permanently." At Nadia's slight shudder, he mentally kicked himself. His harsh tone must've conveyed the violence of the outcome.

"But your poor eye." The princess clucked her distress. "Three months on and you're still not healed."

"I'll be fine. And the eye patch gets me lots of female attention." He kept his expression guarded as he stowed his chewing gum in his cheek. He turned to Nadia. "The DARK assistant director assigned me to light duty until my eye heals. I owe the princess and her father for unchaining me from a desk. Even with half of twenty-twenty, I'm good to go."

Apart from Nadia's resentment of his very presence, the adrenaline rush and challenge of an op was what he needed. He'd have the rebel traitor in the bag in a few days. After this, the AD would see it his way and put him back in the field. Freedom. His soul needed to be back out there. The tightness in his chest was merely due to his need to protect the princess.

Sarika laughed, then turned to Nadia. "Let me explain why my father specifically requested Matt's help. Three years ago during a rebel uprising, this brave and resourceful man saved my life."

Nadia's lips stretched into a tight smile.

Odd, but at that moment the two women looked similar. Had to be the blonde effect. "Just lucky we made it." He looked away, rubbed knuckles across his jaw.

Crossing her ankles, she jiggled one foot. "You must tell me about the rescue sometime, Sari."

"The rebels have regrouped. You may have read about their recent skirmishes with our *garda* patrols. I need your cooperation while Matt's undercover in the embassy."

He added, "The rebels intend to overthrow Modena's parliamentary government and install their own leader, likely Sandor Cardona, an ousted member of parliament."

Nadia's smile vanished as the impact sank in. "As what, a dictatorship?"

"That's our assumption. They've spread propaganda about repression and embezzlement. Apparently they intend to stage a coup by assassinating the royal family as well as the prime minister. Attempts against King Bernard came close. Two members of parliament died in the latest attack. His majesty fears for his only daughter's life."

"The rebels are *here*, in Washington?" Nadia said. "Sari, we'll postpone the film. You can go somewhere safe."

The princess shook her head and smoothed her skirt. "I'll not concede to these vermin who want to destroy my island. Your film will show the truth about Modena."

Now they were getting to the reason for this meeting—his role in Nadia's documentary about the royal family. When Matt had first met her, she'd only just begun her filmmaking career. Now as a producer-director, she had three indie documentaries under her belt. Damned good ones. He'd made a point of streaming them.

"Someone in the embassy is plotting with the rebels," he continued. "No one there is above suspicion, the reason for our meeting in the limo and not in an embassy office. My job is to identify the traitor. Sarika's life is at stake." He checked out the rear window when they stopped for a traffic light.

What he saw put an end to his explanation and sent his blood pressure skyrocketing. A black luxury SUV. The behemoth's wide metal grill loomed close enough to bite the limo's bumper. The saber-tooth-tiger growl of its 420-horsepower engine implied more than tailgating.

"It's probably nothing," Sarika said, oblivious to the SUV. "My father tends to be overprotective."

Wham!

A jolt from behind jerked the two women forward into their shoulder harnesses. Sarika gasped and Nadia emitted a small shriek.

Chapter Two

MATT'S HEAD BOUNCED into the padding below the privacy panel. The impact threw the limo toward the car ahead. The chauffeur slammed on the brakes and avoided a collision.

"The idiot needs a driving lesson," Nadia blurted, settling again. "The one on courtesy of the road."

"I don't think courtesy's the issue." Matt's mouth tightened. Were the SUV guys Modena rebels? Or just jerks having some fun after downing their breakfast brewskis? "We're about to find out if His Majesty's overprotective or right on target."

A big man, tall and wide, a tank like his vehicle, sat with both hands on the steering wheel. Another man, not as big, filled the passenger seat. Both smiled. Not friendly smiles, more the smirks of predators closing in on their prey.

Nadia had twisted around, so she saw the thugs. Her frightened gaze now found Matt's.

As much as he figured she must hate the idea, she would have to rely on him. "Hang on."

He pushed the button for the intercom. "Stefan, are you a good enough driver to lose the SUV crawling up our ass?"

"I used to be, sir, but my reactions are not what they once were." The old man's voice quavered and broke.

Thunk. Thunk. Thunk.

The fuckers were shooting at them. Not just your average street punks, but the rebels. Or worse.

Sarika's eyes widened. She was clearly shaken by a sound too reminiscent of the last time she was under fire. Nadia sucked in a breath and gripped the armrest.

Matt couldn't see the weapon. Probably a suppressor-equipped semi-auto. Anything bigger would be too obvious in public. He had to get off these slow suburban streets. No time to stow the chewing gum, so he swallowed it. He pushed a button. The privacy panel slid down out of sight between the rear-facing seat and the driver compartment. "You two get down on the floor."

"But—" Nadia began.

"Do it now."

The light changed. The big vehicle's engine revved. The delivery van ahead barely moved as gears ground and acrid smoke billowed. The limo and the SUV pulled out as if linked by a short chain.

The women slid to the floor, Nadia behind the passenger seat, the princess beside her.

"We'll be all right," Sarika said, her voice abnormally high pitched. "Matt will handle things. Trust him."

In this case, Nadia had no choice. He stripped off his sport coat. Wrenched away the driver's headrest and tossed it over her head onto the backseat.

"I'm taking the wheel." He directed Stefan to move out of the way.

He held onto the support handle as he drew up his legs. Then he twisted and slid through to the driver compartment. The smaller man scooted across the console, damned fast for an old guy. Matt dropped into the seat and took the wheel.

More bullets rammed into the rear end.

Plastic shattered. Tail light.

The entrance to Cabin John Park appeared on the right, then the sign for I-495. The Capital Beltway, exactly what he needed. This engine had about the same power as the higher SUV but the limo—not a stretch, *grazie*—should have more maneuverability.

At the beltway entrance, he hung a right and sped onto the north ramp. Because of his blind left side, he had to turn his head farther and rely more on the mirrors. He turned enough to glance in the left outside mirror with his right eye, then swung back to see forward. He whipped out into the flow of traffic, heavy as usual but not rush-hour jammed at mid-morning.

Other drivers blasted him with their horns, but he stomped on the gas.

The women huddled behind him. Their movements and hushed words told him they were hanging in there. Beside him, Stefan perched upright and stiff. Matt could smell the sour odor of his fear. Or maybe he smelled his own.

The bastards followed. It took the on-ramp, pulled into traffic two cars behind.

His adrenaline spiked as he accelerated with the traffic flow. He hoped vehicles packed into five lanes, like racers on a track, would shield them. He cranked the limo's eight cylinders.

When the space behind him opened up, the monstrous SUV swerved around and pulled up behind.

What the hell were they doing? Aiming to kill the princess? Maybe kidnap her? Not at high speed for sure, but… He gunned it and the SUV accelerated along with him. It again rammed their rear end.

The limo hopped forward, then veered sideways. The blow nearly bounced them into the left lane.

Into a car he hadn't seen.

Horns blared. He sucked in a deep breath past the vise clamping his chest. The muscles in his shoulders and arms screamed with the strain but he held the limo in the right lane. *Dammit. Damn my eye.* Turning his head too far around meant taking his good eye off the road. Not good.

He needed a freaking guide dog. He hated it but the choice of words was apt. "Nadia, Sarika, the damn eye injury fucks with my vision on the left. Using the mirrors helps but I need one of you to be my eyes."

"I can do it." Nadia's voice was strained. Trying for confidence. "Sarika needs to stay down."

"I'll get out of your way," the princess said. Clothing rustled, shoe soles scraped on the floor mat as the two women switched places.

If only he could see on his left. "Nadia?"

"I'm ready, right behind you. Steady line of cars on the left. Yellow convertible leading the pack."

Matt stayed on course with her keeping him alerted. A solid chain of cars and trucks cruised along, intent on the endless merry-go-round, leaving exhaust fumes in their wake. No one around them seemed to notice what was going on. Where was a cop car when you needed one?

The green thicket of the park grounds sped by on the right, trees stretching above walls erected to block traffic noises. In tandem, the limo and the SUV zoomed past River Road and toward the next exit. The road widened to five lanes for the left-hand I-270 split, so he had to make his move.

"I'm gonna ease left for the exit. Then fake him out."

"I don't get what you're doing, but okay." Nadia's voice sounded strained, but her tone determined. "Blue van pulling in beside you."

He swung back into the right lane just in time.

"Now it's clear. Go."

He whipped the car left. The pursuer still hung in the right lane. Then it found an opening and veered into his but remained two cars behind. Good. "Again?"

She told him to wait for a semi to pass. The split for the northern suburbs was fast approaching. The other vehicle moved closer again as another car edged right. Only one car back.

He was running out of time. He gripped the steering wheel tighter.

"Okay, go," Nadia said.

He peeled to his left as if headed for Gaithersburg, luring the SUV to follow. He gunned it to get clear.

A delivery van blocked the SUV. Here was his chance. He'd done this once on the Autobahn, but that time he was doing the chasing. And he had vision in both eyes. "Everybody hold onto something. This could be hairy."

No time or energy to spend on worrying. He ripped the wheel to the right and knifed through vehicles across the right hand lanes headed east around the beltway.

"The SUV?" He slowed to blend into traffic in the far right lane.

"He's coming." He could hear panic shredding her voice. "Oh, God, we didn't shake him. What can we do?"

"How far back is he?" Matt didn't dare turn to see. Vehicles were speeding bumper to bumper at seventy and higher.

"About ten cars. Maybe more. But in the fast lane."

He could still do it. Even if the bastards spotted them exiting. "I'm going into Bethesda again. I can lose him on back streets." At least that was his plan.

Chapter Three

MATT WRENCHED THE wheel a hard right and sped down the exit ramp. He hugged the arc of the exit curve. His best chance here was that he knew the tangled streets. Likely their pursuers did not.

This early in the morning, traffic on Old Georgetown Road bustled with more delivery trucks than cars. Before the dickwads could catch up or figure out where the limo had gone, he had to get invisible. He scooted around a semi backing into a Dunkin, then careened right onto a side street.

No sign of the monster SUV.

More random twists and turns took them through a neighborhood of older Colonials, and then he swung into a school parking lot. He stopped behind the second row of vehicles. Nobody followed them. The women were safe. He rotated his shoulders and drew a breath, flexed his aching fingers. His heart rate began to ease up.

Stefan heaved a giant sigh. "You lost them. In my day, I could have done that." Beaming a wide and gap-toothed smile, the chauffeur clapped Matt on the back.

****

Nadia sank to the limo floor and drew deep breaths. She folded her arms and pressed them against her stomach, a vain attempt to ease the emotions rocking her. Her pulse still fluttered.

She glanced at her friend. Pale blond strands of

Sari's always perfect hair had come loose from her chignon, and she'd chewed off her lipstick. About like Nadia must look. Maybe more shaken. Sari hadn't wanted to believe the rebels would really attack her. Her chest rose and fell with a shudder, and she sent Nadia a wobbly smile. What the hell was going on? Rebels ramming them, shooting at them to kill the princess? The world had gone crazy.

The motor was still running, but the front door locks clicked. Stefan opened the passenger-side door. Clucking his tongue, he aided the princess to exit. When Matt opened the door beside Nadia and held out a hand, she hesitated. Not letting him help her would be petty, especially after he probably saved *all* their lives, not just Sari's. The touch of his fingers as he supported her shot electric vibrations up her arm, and the berry scent of his chewing gum tickled memories she'd suppressed.

"You okay?"

She pulled her hand from his and nodded, not trusting her vocal cords for speech.

"Take your time." He reached inside the limo to the mini-fridge, then handed her a bottle of water. "Then we'll head for the embassy."

"Police?"

His brows drew together, the expression rendered fierce because of the scar bisecting the left one. A muscle twitched in his strong jaw. "I'd rather not call in the cops, but it'll look fishy if we don't. The limo's rear end took a few hits, remember?"

On a shudder, she said, "How could I forget?"

"Better if Sarika makes the call, but after we make it to the embassy."

Nadia dragged in giant gulps of the fresh air before

letting the cold liquid soothe her sandy throat. Her knees quivered like saplings in a storm. She leaned against the car door and pressed the bottle to her forehead.

Matt left with a water bottle for the princess, his stride unhurried but somehow predatory.

She never thought she'd say it but thank God for him. He'd climbed into the front seat, the fastest she'd ever seen the man move. His normal speed was slo-mo. Men had been shooting at them, but he never flinched. His outrageous driving brought them to safety. She shivered to dispel her unwanted admiration.

Having him pop up like a discarded video file renewed all her anger from five years ago. Seeing him lounging beside Sarika, of all people, had pulled her back in time. Into the old resentment. And the old attraction.

An attraction she could control, even with him in the embassy. She'd be too busy with the filming to run into him.

Rebels. Undercover work. Anxiety sifted through her belly.

She drank water. All was quiet. No one had apparently noticed the strange vehicle amid the other cars. The sight of paper jack-o'-lanterns decorating the windows of the redbrick building comforted her. Ordinary. Sane.

Nadia was a mass of fractured nerve endings. Not the others. The diminutive chauffeur stood at attention as always. Sarika was talking to Matt on the other side of the limo. She looked serene in her now-wrinkled silk ecru suit as if nothing unusual had happened, her hair back in place. A few years younger than Matt, she was Nadia's age of thirty. An exotic beauty with bold features in an oval face.

Other than the sweat stains marring Matt's dress shirt and a few finger-track lines in his short black hair, he looked as if today's bullet-riddled chase was par for the course. And maybe it was. For him. Blue jeans, no tie, of course. Signature Leoni. His solid, muscular build had made her feel protected.

Thin red scars slashed his left eyebrow and the cheekbone below the black eye patch. Shrapnel from a bomb? Or a terrorist's knife? She shuddered. Whatever happened in that incident might explain the new edge she sensed in him. Harshness, a guarded tension. He was a more dangerous man than she'd realized before.

She'd fallen for him, first for his dark eyes, square-jawed solidity and deep voice, then for his wry humor and sexy, sleepy demeanor that hid a sharp brain.

But then he'd used her to trap her father. She could never forgive him. His betrayal twisted through her stomach.

Neither could she abandon her friend. Or her film. Her company needed the gig, the money. She needed to complete the film with no hitches. She'd already spent most of the Today's World Network advance.

****

Matt couldn't prevent himself from flinching as Nadia whirled on him.

"You as part of my film crew? You may be a top-notch Fed but you know zip about films or filming. Sari must be so scared she's not thinking straight." She paced the tan wall-to-wall carpet. "Look, I'm sorry about your eye injury. My feelings about all this—" she gestured at the room assigned to Monte Cristo Productions "—are obvious, but I don't wish you harm. I hope your vision will be fine."

He nodded but couldn't manage a smile. "I appreciate that. Fifty-fifty chance, but I'm hopeful." The knot just below his sternum wound tight as ever. Hell, fifty percent was damned good odds. He'd heal. Like the doc said, not a problem. Temporary. Wouldn't affect his work. He wouldn't let it.

She stomped to the door. "I have to check on something. I don't need to tell you to make yourself at home. You will anyway. I'll be back in ten, fifteen minutes." She slammed out, except the door closed itself silently, which probably pissed her off even more.

Matt got why she was still steaming after Sarika had explained his undercover role. She probably needed some time to adjust. *Let her yell at me. As long as she agrees to the arrangement.*

And as long as she didn't blow his cover. During the police interview she'd held tough. A good sign.

Crime techs photographed the limo's damage and extracted the bullets. The detective had written down their narration of the attack. Before he left, he berated them all for driving to the embassy before calling. In his film-crew persona, Matt had replied that everybody was too scared to do anything else.

He strolled around the film company's HQ, rotating his shoulders to appear to be getting out the kinks as he scanned for cameras. The jacket was tight. Must be the work-outs due to his frustration at being confined to a desk.

This room was in the basement, a disused clerical office, judging from the carpet imprints of cubicles and the electrical connections. A stack of metal chairs jammed up a corner of the space, which was little bigger than his one-bed condo.

Two metal tables were pushed together in an L. A take-out food container with a lingering teriyaki smell, printouts, and a tablet littered the surface beside a red leather tote. Nadia always carried purses big enough to be overnight bags. His gaze lit on earbuds beside a granola bar. Did she still listen to Bruno Mars?

No cameras. He took out his bug detector, a miniature unit in ballpoint-pen form designed by one of the DARK techs, and cruised the office again. No listening devices. Either Sarika had ordered the filming headquarters sacrosanct or else neither Modena Embassy Security nor the rebels' man saw Nadia as a threat.

He sank onto a folding chair at one of the tables. He slid off the eye patch and tossed it on the table. Damn thing was hot, itched something fierce. Propping his feet on a box of copy paper, he pondered the possibilities. The uniformed branch of the U.S. Secret Service provided external protection for larger countries' embassies, not for small countries like Modena. And not wanting to alienate those Modenans sympathetic to their cause, the rebels weren't plotting against the entire embassy, only against the princess, so their attack would be personal. The reason they needed insider intel.

He took out his phone, tapped the coded number for his DARK contact.

"Leoni, what took you so long to check in? You just wake up from a nap?"

Matt grinned. Like Cole Stratton didn't know what was going on. The ex-Marine never missed a detail or a nuance, always had up-to-date intel. "Very funny. Chilling helps me process. You should try it sometime, Jarhead."

"Oo-rah." Stratton could stand to chill. He never

stopped working except when the two of them put their Harleys through their paces. "How's Hollywood East? Can't be too bad if Nadia Parker hasn't bumped you off."

He might as well launch into his report. "It wasn't her doing the shooting. Surveillance get a good view of the limo when we pulled in?"

"Like you don't know. Smashed taillight, some bullet holes in the chassis."

Matt described in detail the chase, the thugs, the gunshots, and their route. He omitted Nadia's part in helping navigate his escape maneuvers. Might catch flak for that, but he didn't want to deal with that now. It shouldn't matter after this gig ended in success. A knot tightened in his gut to compete with the one in his chest.

"And the women?"

"Shaken up but fine. Can't say the cops were pleased we waited so long to report the attack. I wanted the princess and Nadia away from Bethesda in case the scumbags were still hanging around."

Matt heard another voice in the background. Then Stratton said, "Simon Byrne wants to know how you're doing with the sexy producer."

Matt shrugged. "Nadia's resisting. We'll see. You guys must be laughing your asses off at the irony of me working with her."

"A few yuks, yeah. Just watch your back. Hey, can you do that with one eye?"

"With one eye and one hand if I had to." Damn, he hoped he didn't sound too pissed off.

"Saw you on the firing range yesterday. Improving your percentage."

As his friend's statement registered, he jerked upright. Stratton had been paying attention. For the big honchos? Or just as his friend? Matt was left handed and left eyed. Sighting with his right eye meant relearning and retraining muscles. Hell, retraining his brain. "I'll be back up to regs soon. Just takes practice." And the current problem took precedence. "Any clues who the rebel leader has sent?"

"Chatter on the Internet but nothing concrete," Stratton said. "Could be the leader himself. Don't know how Cardona could've gotten into the country. Could've slipped across the Canadian border."

Sandor Cardona. Matt's experience four years ago told him Cardona was a hands-on guy. He would coordinate assassinations in person, maybe even take part. "Modena has plenty of security. Their *garda* force is known to be damned sharp. So this op must be more than a favor to Director Nolan's old friend the king. Modena's a small island—wealthy, for damn sure. Its location halfway between Italy and North Africa makes it a plum grab for outside agitators. Even terrorists. Another reason for DARK's involvement?"

"Affirmative. Cardona has ties to a terrorist group in Yamar with big ambitions," Byrne said.

"Must be New Dawn again." He grimaced. The mission resulting in his eye injury involved those bastards. "If rumors are true that they get funding from Russia, no wonder the king's worried."

"According to our boss, His Majesty discounts the terrorist connection. Insists Modenans might want a change of ruler, but they'd never betray their country by turning it over to terrorists."

"Naïve." Matt turned over in his mind what else he knew about Modena. "During the Cold War, the U.S. established a naval base with an air field on the island's eastern end. They turned it over to Modena years ago, but Special Forces land for supplies and our ships refuel there. A base like that would be a mighty big carrot. A rebel coup could drop that naval base into New Dawn's hands—a tragedy for Modena and a disaster of incredible proportions for everyone."

"You move slow but you think fast," Stratton said. "So get off your ass and find that traitor in the embassy. And Princess Sarika may be optimistic about there being only one."

"Copy that. Who knows how many others Cardona and company have gotten to? Anyone might be an assassin. Or a paid assassin."

A rattle of paper. "Hold on."

Another voice was quickly muffled by a hand over the receiver.

A binder lay on the table with "Monte Cristo Productions-Modena Embassy" on it. Nadia always did prefer printouts to scrolling down a screen. While he waited, he smiled and browsed through the contents. Location images—the embassy, personnel in the corridors, views of the street, the Capitol Building—all labeled. Other pages of the embassy's website and news reports. The woman was thorough.

A sheet of paper slid out. Below the Monte Cristo heading was a scribbled list.

Refugees/migrants. Modena & Greece. Mobile health care for the homeless. Dallas.

Future film contracts? Or a wish list? If so, she still intended to make socially conscious documentaries, one of the things he admired about her. She was warmhearted, wanting to make documentaries that could lead to improvement in people's lives.

A click and Stratton's voice in his ear. "One more thing, Leoni. Stick close to Parker."

The hairs stood up on his nape. He knew what *stick close* really meant. He slammed his feet to the floor. "I'm to fucking *spy* on her?" When the other man didn't respond, he said, "That's not part of the op. Nadia was never implicated in her father's crimes. She's clean. Never even suspected." By most, by anybody who counted.

Again the voice in the background. This time Matt recognized the low tones of the DARK director, General Nolan.

His muscles tightened. "Work with me here."

On a deep sigh, Stratton said, "The director just shared new data. Here's the deal, Leoni. If Yamari terrorists are behind this and the Kremlin's funding them, the rebels have big money. Parker needs bucks for another court appeal. She's susceptible."

His heart knocked several slow and painful thumps. "Nadia would never betray Princess Sarika. They're friends." He gripped the binder hard enough to pop knuckles.

"Green's a powerful motivator. Keeping an eye on Parker is only a precaution."

Pain drilled into his chest. How could he refuse? This op was his ticket back to field service. Back to the challenge, back to having this weight off his chest. Nadia would hate him even more if she found out he was spying on her. "Is that an order?"

"Affirmative."

Chapter Four

MATT LOOKED UP from the film binder when Nadia flung open the door.

"I agreed to this arrangement only because I want to help Sari. And I owe her." She stopped dead, shoulders rigid, her eyes flashing green fire. A good bet she'd been arguing with the princess about his undercover role. She tilted her head, and her gaze softened. "You're not wearing your eye patch. Don't you need it for protection?"

Dammit, he'd forgotten. He shook his head. How could he explain? *Take the easy route.* "Yeah, but it's hot. Itchy." Which was true, as far as it went. He snatched up the black demon and snapped it in place. "Satisfied?"

"Not even close, but it seems I'm stuck with you."

Working with her wouldn't be any easier on him than on her. For now he had to forge a truce so this undercover gig would fly. He joined her on the other side of the metal table. "We might as well lay out the real issue. I get that you resent the hell out of my presence."

Nadia folded her arms beneath her breasts. Only a few inches shorter than his six feet, she didn't have to look up much to glare at him.

He tugged his gaze up from the cleavage in her V-neck to meet her eyes. "My being here isn't why you're angry. Investigating your father was DARK's job. *My duty.*"

She tapped one foot on the carpet. Her eyes glistened with emotion. "But why the Domestic Antiterrorism Risk Corps, as if my father was a terrorist?" She swiped away moisture. "Dad's not one, but he did sell documents *to* terrorists, I concede that. But I don't know why."

What? The trial didn't bring out his motives, but her dad had never explained it to his only daughter? Now wasn't the time to ask.

She shook her head as if shaking away the trauma remembering had brought back. "Was your Romeo act also part of your *duty*? Was everything you told me a lie? Like the foster care and the group home?"

He'd forgotten he'd shared that with her. DARK officials knew, but he never told anyone casually. Other people had families. He didn't. "No act. I never lied to you. Everything I said to you was true. My parents... died. I was a kid. And I did grow up in foster care and a group home."

She huffed as if she still didn't believe him. During the investigation, he hadn't been able to stay away from her. Kisses, fooling around, hot words. He lost count of his cold showers. But having sex with her would've crossed a professional line. And his personal line. That he'd wanted her and held back burned a fuse through him now.

He heaved a sigh. "My interest in you had nothing to do with DARK. I hung out with you because I liked you. I admired your loyalty to your dad, no matter what. Beyond that, the attraction was real—hormones, desire, sex—not pure but simple. I never meant to hurt you. I apologize." She probably didn't believe him. He still liked her and admired her, but she wouldn't believe that either.

When they'd found the damning evidence that led to her father's arrest, he felt rotten. He wanted to tell her the truth then, but DARK ordered him not to contact her. He hadn't wanted to jeopardize the case. Or his career. He needed DARK. Now the omission sat in his belly like an anvil.

She didn't respond, only turned away and plopped onto the chair at her computer. "I have to check e-mail." She pressed a key. An email program popped up, covering the desktop image of an island tower. The logo of Monte Cristo Productions, he assumed, gritting his teeth at the irony of her choice. She tapped keys.

He liked her voice and watching her expressive eyes as emotions chased across her face—even when she fired both barrels at him. He homed in on her creamy skin, her dark lashes, and the smooth column of her neck. Her lush mouth thinned as she tapped furiously on the keyboard. She'd kicked off her shoes.

The sight of her toenails painted hot pink sent a shimmer of sensation to his groin. Damn. He was in trouble if even her toes turned him on. He'd had the same reaction to her when they first met. He'd been with a few women since then, but none who jazzed him like Nadia. His desire for her had intensified as he got to know her. She crackled with vitality and passion.

Would she focus all that juice on a man in bed? On him? Not a chance in hell he'd find out.

Five years ago she'd concentrated on her commitment to her old man. Looked like she still did if she was raising funds for his appeal and not for her ambition. Family loyalty was admirable, although misplaced here. Isaac Parker, a graphic artist illustrating technical manuals for intelligence agencies, had sold government secrets to a splinter group of Al-Qaida. Lying to his daughter until his guilt became too obvious to hide lowered the man to fungus status. And Matt had added to her pain.

He'd like to prove to her she could trust him, convince her he hadn't used her to get the goods on her old man.

But what would be the point? Even if she could forgive him, he saw no real chance of them picking up where they'd left off. Would she go for a long weekend together, dinners and hot sex? Because that's all he could offer any woman. He'd grown up without control over his life and wouldn't give up his freedom for anyone. No matter what happened with his vision.

She'd have to talk to him soon to show him the ropes. He didn't want to push her but time was short. Made shorter by today's attack. Neither DARK nor Sarika knew how much time they had to flush out the damn mole and worm out of him the rebels' other plans.

She'd had a rough morning. *Give her a minute. Or two.* He sank onto the other desk chair at the table.

Nadia couldn't focus on the screen in front of her. She hated this storm of emotions inside her. His hesitant words about foster care, barely above a whisper, and his shuttered expression meant the story was true. Did that mean the rest was true—that he'd genuinely liked her and wanted her? If he was waiting for her to confess she'd felt the same until he'd betrayed her, he'd have to wait into the next century. Dammit, she didn't want to feel this awareness of him. Or this anger at him. Or this sympathy for him. Or this confusion over which emotion made her heart pound like a runaway locomotive.

She was stuck with him, wasn't she? For as long as it took to find the traitor. He was here only to keep Sari safe. She could handle it. She could.

But she needed this segment of the film to be a go—without much delay. King Bernard wanted the entire documentary in the can by winter. His PR offensive, he'd told Sari. Even spring would be a tall order, given all that would have to be filmed and edited once in Modena. Then she needed time and leisure to look for her mom's family. If any existed. Why wouldn't Mom ever talk about them? Or Dad? Was she ashamed of them?

A sneaked glance at Matt sent warmth up her spine. He reclined with a casual grace that set her blood humming. His eyes—eye, the one she could see, was half closed. Sleepy. Sexy. Seductive.

To stop her foot tapping she crossed her ankles.

He always seemed to move in low gear. Or was it a dangerous calm, part of his duplicity? How did he keep those powerful biceps and the broad chest and shoulders? Fighting bad guys? Chasing terrorists?

Since she couldn't concentrate on the email from the network, she might as well get more answers. "What does your undercover gig here entail? How will it affect filming?"

"My presence in your crew gives me access to embassy people, the chance to talk to some and observe." She'd never considered a Boston accent sexy, but in Matt's baritone, the clipped inflection danced along her spine. "I'm here to identify the traitor, not take him down. As long as my cover as the documentary writer holds, you and your crew are in no danger. In spite of what happened this morning."

Danger? His presence already endangered her sanity. She barely refrained from rolling her eyes. "That's so comforting to know."

He leaned forward, his forearms resting on his knees. "Nadia, what you did was brave. Acting as my lookout at the window put you in the line of fire."

She fought the warmth his words kindled. She never would've expected praise. Along with indolence, the man possessed ego and arrogance. Leoni, aptly named for the king of the beasts. She suppressed a grin. "Sari's my friend. I want to protect her as much as you do."

"Sari, not *Princess Sarika*. How'd you become friends?"

"Your DARK spying didn't tell you?"

"I know a lot about you. Not this. Care to explain?"

No reason not to. "I've known her since I was little."

"Through your mom?"

Her mom had died too young. Only months after giving Nadia her first camera for her twelfth birthday. She had to swallow before she could reply. "My mom was born in a small town on Modena. She worked for the royal family before she came to the States, was close to Sarika's mother before she became queen. The two women phoned a lot when Sari and I were little—she's six months older—sometimes about us girls. After Mom died, the queen continued to keep in touch, and Sari and I emailed almost daily. When we studied at GW, we shared an apartment. She was instrumental in getting this film job for my company."

"I'll try not to screw things up too bad for you." He lowered his feet to the floor and turned toward her. "Sarika said you were short on staff. Problem?"

She tucked her hair behind her ears. "Indie

filmmaking is competitive. Skilled crew migrates with the money." And she couldn't offer big. Or close to big. "Anyway, the embassy limited me to four personnel, including me. Security reasons. For this segment of the shoot, a small crew will do."

"You're producer-director. That's one. You lost guys to another company. That it?" He propped his left elbow on the table and edged his chair closer.

Too close. His scent swept her with longing—gum, spearmint this time, and faint perspiration, a remnant of that horrible car chase. He'd told her once that he'd taken up gum chewing as a sort of defense. He didn't want to waste what little money he had on smokes the others in his group home would cadge or steal. Given his earlier hesitant confession, she supposed that story might also be true. How sad. She wanted to ask him more about his parents. *But no, cut off the sympathy, the nostalgia.* Was he manipulating her again? She crossed her legs and let one foot jiggle. She should back up but the other table blocked her.

"Ken Burns is starting a new six-part miniseries. Anyone not already contracted elsewhere headed his way. And my usual DP—that's director of photography, a fancy term for cameraman—and the sound tech, his wife, had a car accident yesterday in Chicago. Drunk driver, I think. They're out."

"Injuries bad?"

Tears swarmed in her eyes and she blinked them back. "Concussion, maybe broken bones. They'll mend. But it's so criminal. Jamal and Vivian were pumped about this gig."

"They're your friends."

Perceptive of him, drat the man. About the only real

friends she had, moving from gig to gig as she did. Maintaining relationships was a tough order, and not just with friends. She'd lost a fiancé and chances with other men. No way would she include Matt in that assessment. Emotion squeezed her chest. "Yes."

"I'm sorry. So that leaves you with only me?"

Thankfully, no. She almost sighed in relief. "I found replacements online. I don't know how good these two guys are, but they're here in the city. They start tomorrow."

Concern flickered in his eyes. For her or for his mission, she couldn't guess. "So what job do you have for me in addition to writer?"

She'd mulled that over during the walk back after complaining to Sari. Much as it galled her. She wound her legs together to stop the damn twitching. "This segment of the documentary is more manageable than it will be on Modena. Mostly interviews, walk-and-talks, B-rolls in the embassy."

"B-rolls? Is that lunch?"

Refusing to take the bait, she bit her lower lip. She would *not* let him charm her. Not this time. On a huffed sigh, she said, "B-rolls are anything other than interviews. Voice-overs are dubbed in later."

Shifting in her seat, she drummed the fingers of her right hand on the table.

"How about best boy? I've always wanted to be the best boy." Mischief gleamed gold in his dark gaze. His mouth curved, waking his dimples and sucking the air from her lungs.

Since she couldn't speak, she frowned.

When she didn't bite, he shrugged. "So what am I doing? Sound assistant? Lighting assistant?"

"The DP does his own lighting." Matt would grasp technical skills in no time. But nuances and artistry came only with experience. "For now, you're the production assistant, otherwise known as the *grip*. For you that means anything extra, like moving equipment. Manning the boom mic. Setting up once you know how. No one, not even the new guys will question that the writer would need training to double as grip."

"I'm cool with that. So what's next?"

"Um, I have pre-production work. Scheduling interviews, the script, stuff like that. Mostly things to finalize." Too inane. Next she'd start to babble.

A glance at the yellow pad by her elbow reminded her of another chore. "The camera and sound guys will have their own equipment, but I have to place an order for lighting, cables, and other equipment. Then I have to pick it all up."

"Ordering stuff is something a new production assistant can do without training as long as you have a list and the website or a phone number. Unless you have some training in mind? Or something I can *grip*?" He waggled his eyebrows, to startling effect, given the scars and the pirate patch.

No, she would *not* think of him as a pirate.

He was so close she could see the gold rim in his slumberous eye. Awareness filtered into her every pore, sapping her resistance. He bent closer, twirled a finger in a tendril of her hair.

Was he going to kiss her?

She knew the heat of his mouth on hers, the taste of his tongue and the strength of his arms around her. Her traitorous body wanted those sensations again. And more.

She should push away. Protest. Probably. Positively.

Chapter Five

LATER, AFTER MATT had ordered and collected the rental equipment, Nadia took him through the building. Either she wasn't as affected by their near-kiss as he was or she was a damned good actress. She breezed along the corridors, describing the offices, conference rooms, and personnel in them. He'd already studied all the locations and staff and had most memorized, but her guiding allowed him to absorb more details.

She'd have let him kiss her. He'd seen it in the tilt of her head and the darkening of her eyes. But he figured she might misinterpret the move, or resent it, so he'd turned away and got to his feet. Maybe her nonchalance as they toured meant she was relieved. Ken Ritter, one of the DARK officers on the Isaac Parker investigation, had claimed then that she came on to Matt only to sidetrack him. He didn't buy it. Her kisses, her sighs, her touches… She'd meant all of that as much as he had.

He should forget his fascination with her and concentrate on the damn traitor, whoever he was. Preventing harm to Sarika was his mission, nothing else. So why did his belly clench like when he'd waked up to the disastrous outcome of that Brussels explosion?

Better to concentrate on the building. Because of annexing two neighboring houses, the place was a rabbit warren. Carved wooden doors led to offices—first floor clerical and Security, second and third for higher-level diplomatic staff. Brass nameplates for all offices. The fourth floor was storage, and the basement held the Monte Cristo quarters, a kitchen, and a dining hall.

People carrying folders or tablets or both bustled along the corridors, which crisscrossed, their walls in a soft green. He caught conversations in Italian, French, and English, three of Modena's national languages. Only Greek was missing. A few smiled and nodded, but others broadcast only cool dismissal—or even outright disdain—like he was something scraped off the soles of their polished shoes. Could be his eye patch made him look too unsavory, a reason for mistrust. Or they simply disapproved of the film project.

As they passed a set of double doors on the third floor, Nadia gestured to the larger nameplate. "Ambassador Vincenzo will be one of our interviews, but today she's giving a speech at American University. If we run into any of the attachés, I'll introduce you."

"*Signorina* Parker, does this *person* have Modena Security clearance?" The voice was part gravel and part Rottweiler.

"Ah, Captain, how lovely," Nadia wheeled, flashing a smile that heated the hallway in general—and Matt specifically. "I was hoping we'd run into you. Yes, indeed, Matt Rikard, my script writer, has the clearance you yourself authorized." She turned to Matt. "Meet the esteemed Captain Renzo, head of Modena Embassy Security. He keeps us all safe. And on our toes."

The security chief looked like he sounded. On his days off, he could moonlight as an MMA fighter, minus the 9mm currently at his waist. Matt gave a small nod of greeting, waited for the other man to extend a hand. He didn't.

33

Renzo's gaze was cold, wary. And pointed, like a bayonet. If anybody could out Matt as an interloper, it would be this man. Matt could've matched his dead-eyed cop stare, but schooled his expression into mild-mannered, creative film guy.

One black eyebrow arched as the security chief turned to Nadia. "Yet another crew member, *Signorina* Parker?"

She drew in a quick breath. Matt wanted to tuck her behind him. Hell, his body wanted more than that, but he stood by. This was her show. "But sir, you approved Matt days ago, remember? He's doubling as production assistant. Only one in my crew, plus me, I assure you."

The chill in Renzo's eyes didn't thaw, and the corners of his mouth turned downward. He grunted in acknowledgment. He'd forgotten. Probably had wanted to swing his self-important weight around and now would cover his blunder. "Him I remember. Then you needed new ones."

"My apologies for taking up your valuable time. I appreciate your vetting my other crew members on such short notice. King Bernard is so eager to have this film completed soon, I will certainly tell him about your efforts in behalf of my little company."

Damn, but she was good. The hint of flirtation in her wide smile, an added sweetener, brought spots of color high on the man's cheeks.

He threw back his shoulders. "Very well, proceed. *Signorina*, Rikard." Matt expected him to click his heels together, but he executed a sharp turn and strode away down the corridor.

She blew out a breath. "For a minute I thought we were in trouble."

"Nah, you turned that confrontation totally around in your favor. You could be a diplomat." On a chuckle, he added, "Matt Rikard, the script writer. I like the sound of that."

"Don't let it go to your head." They reached the elevator, and before she could push the button, it opened and disgorged three people.

When they exited on the second floor, she gestured to an open lounge on their left, where two people were deep in conversation. Sarika smiled at something the man was saying. "That's Dominic Traynor, the prime minister's emissary. He accompanies her on most of the trade talks." Nadia lowered her voice. She chuckled. "Usually I see him stalking along the corridors and hovering in doorways with a scowl, a brooding expression. But I think he has a thing for his princess."

Matt recognized him. Tall, aristocratic, fortyish, wearing a hand-tailored suit that the elite set called bespoke. In his photos he seemed to have a stick up his ass, but not at the moment. As he bent his head toward Sari, his stern features softened. A person of interest, the heading on the file had indicated. But Matt said nothing to Nadia. Damn, he trusted her, but DARK didn't, and she didn't need to know that he already knew some of what she was telling him. Except for Traynor's hall-monitor patrolling and interest in Sarika, which could be real or feigned.

When the princess's admin hurried into the lounge, Matt and Nadia moved on.

Farther down the corridor, she said, "This is the office of George Ingel, the minister of political affairs. He told me he can't wait for the interview. He asked if he needed makeup." She laughed, touching Matt briefly on the arm before she snatched away her hand.

"Forget yourself for a moment, honey?"

She huffed and rolled her eyes.

He grinned to himself as they returned to the documentary's quarters. She *had* forgotten to keep her distance, so maybe her resentment was easing up.

He did recon alone that afternoon. No one paid attention to him as he fiddled with his prop, a light meter, and planted some of the electronics hidden in his sport coat lining. He managed to chat up some of the female staff. Most seemed jazzed at his suggestion they might appear in some of the film's scenes, but he couldn't glean any gossip about dodgy characters.

****

The next day, Nadia's new hires arrived with massive aluminum cases—the cameras and the sound paraphernalia. Hoping his cover story held up, Matt stood quietly while Nadia made the introductions.

Ned Kelmen, the beanpole of a cameraman, didn't look strong enough to wrestle the heavy equipment. The sound tech, Brody Herbert, was a lumpy man in dirty khakis who reeked of tobacco. The two seemed to have worked together before. They accepted Matt as the writer, but seemed doubtful of his ability to perform as grip. Nadia had explained the embassy's crew-size limitations and pointed out he spoke Italian, one of Modena's languages. After a few questions about the eye patch and the scars—a fireworks accident, he told them, damned close to the truth—the new guys eased up on him.

Three days later, after laying cable and setting up light stands in a mahogany-paneled conference room, Matt hustled out of the way as the interview began. He could do the basics without Nadia or the two techs yelling at him. But he was slow and everything was rush, rush, rush. Kelman liked to bark, "Time is money," hourly. By the end of his stint, maybe he'd be down with the jargon. For now it was all geek—full scrims, heads with barn doors, follow-focus. Tripods were *sticks*, and the HD camera had something called a RockNRoll handle. Fortunately, working one-eyed was not a problem.

Although the initial backgrounder declared Kelmen and Herbert legit, a niggling unease told Matt something was off about those two. Although the accident that had hospitalized the original crew seemed designed to substitute ringers, nothing suspicious surfaced, and these guys clearly knew what they were doing. His only recourse was to watch them. But he'd requested a deeper probe into them and the accident.

He returned his focus to the shoot. The interview was winding down. With his round, ruddy face, Minister of Political Affairs George Ingel looked more like a jolly Santa than an opponent of the monarchy. No lean and hungry look on that fat cat. But looks often lied.

Nothing in the DARK reports hinted at anything beyond political maneuvering. Matt would withhold assumptions until he evaluated the results of the electronic bugs and minicams he'd planted and until he sweet-talked the man's blonde admin assistant.

When he wasn't probing the embassy staff, Nadia snagged his attention. The woman had impressive people skills. She'd cheerfully brought the new guys up to speed and charmed everybody they filmed.

She directed the show as well as conducted the interview. Out of camera shot, she sat to the side.

Kelmen's powerful lens framed her subject as he smoothed his black suit.

"Mr. Minister," she said, "what else would you care to share about the stabilizing influence of the royal family?"

"Modena is fortunate to have been ruled by the Constantin family for hundreds of years." Ingel spoke English with the vaguely European accent typical of Modena. His smooth politician's delivery meant he had the bullshit ready before he heard the questions. "Although our parliament and the prime minister conduct most of the governing, the people look to the royal family for continuity and…."

As Ingel droned on, Matt's gaze again drifted to Nadia, who looked hot and as professional as a network anchor in her red jacket and skinny black pants. Professional, yeah, unless you checked her footwear, red cross trainers. Easier to move around with all the cables, she'd told him. Made sense. After the first day, he'd opted for running shoes.

Her anger at his perceived past deceit seemed to have cooled, so the order to spy on her gave him twinges of conscience now and again. He'd installed a keylogger in her laptop, so Stratton and company in DARK headquarters could monitor her typing. Only film-related emails and documents so far. As Matt expected.

Except for working together, she avoided him. Another officer kept surveillance at her hotel. When this was over, any confession would only make her hate him again. And hurt her again. The thought twisted through him. Damn, he hated deceiving her.

The lighting shut down and brought him back to the scene.

Nadia shook Ingel's hand and thanked him. He beamed, his ruddy complexion deepening, and gushed about the film's impact on his country.

Matt unclamped the reflectors and prepared to move the light stands. As he wound up one of the cables, he noticed Ingel's admin, Alina, in the back of the room. Frowning, she held a clipboard, her crimson mouth pursed. With distaste? Dissent? A possibility.

Matt sidled closer. "You disapprove?" he asked in Italian, her native tongue according to intel.

She looked up, startled. "Forgive me. I should not have reacted so. No, the film will show good things about Modena and our royals."

He sent her his best grin, the one that punched in his dimples. "Ah, Alina, that pretty blush must mean something. Your boss, then? It's no secret he thinks the country should eliminate the monarchy."

Fluttering lashes daubed with enough mascara to paint a wall, she made a shushing sound.

"Why do this interview then?" he asked.

"He likes his job. And he likes being on camera."

Before he could probe further, Ingel sailed by and snapped his fingers at her.

She smiled and pushed impressive boobs not created by nature against Matt's side. "Meet me later," she cooed. "We can go out for a drink."

She wasn't his type. Too much make-up. Too much plastic. He made the date anyway. After a few glasses, he might coax her to dish on her boss.

As she wiggled along in her boss's wake, Matt's gaze veered to Ingel's back. Interesting he preferred to do the interview here, not in his office. Was he hiding something? Would he cozy up to terrorists to achieve a revolt? And assassinate the monarchy? Including the only heir, Princess Sarika?

****

Nadia covertly observed Matt that afternoon as they set up to film in Sarika's office. Every nerve ending she possessed sizzled with awareness. She flipped pages on her clipboard to check her prepared questions, but her gaze kept returning to him.

He'd nearly kissed her the other day, and she'd have let him. Dammit, she wanted again the heat of his lips and the sensual textures of tongue and teeth. She'd never forgotten their time together any more than he claimed to. She'd started to think he meant it about his attraction to her. But no more. Today he was hitting on that plastic-Barbie Alina.

Nadia got the picture. Matt hit on any female under fifty. Every female fell for those dimples. And the eye patch added an aura of danger and mystery.

So what? She had no interest in him beyond getting through this ordeal. Yet when Alina rubbed her surgical enhancements against him, she couldn't prevent the twisting and churning inside. She wanted to scream. She wanted to slap him. She wanted—

Hell, she didn't know what she wanted. Why did she let him keep invading her thoughts? *Don't answer that.*

He was running the cables while Kelmen adjusted the camcorder and Herbert tested the princess's microphone. Sarika, the scowling emissary Traynor, and Minister Ingel conferred in front of the bay window where the shoot would take place. Sarika's and Ingel's admins stood by, taking notes on tablets.

In an ice-blue jacket dress, Sarika looked elegant and perfect, as usual. Always the perfectionist, she walked to the gold-framed mirror with her handbag. A moment later, lipstick refreshed and hair tidied, both totally unnecessary, she turned and smiled.

Nadia gave her a thumbs-up and breathed deeply. She had to get her preoccupation with Matt in check before this interview. It would be the centerpiece of the U.S. segment. Monte Cristo Production's film. Her production film. She inhaled the odors of ozone and overheated bodies and hair spray. She loved it all.

Feeling calmer, she returned her gaze to Matt as he set up the light stands. Darned if she wasn't impressed with how he'd dived into his production-assistant role. He ordered all the equipment, including the top-flight lighting Kelmen was maneuvering into place. And for a lower rent than she'd expected to pay.

A wheeler-dealer. Who knew? And today he looked especially fine in a charcoal collared shirt that stretched across powerful shoulders and jeans that—

"Hey, Nadia," Kelmen called. "You want those drapes closed before we start?"

She shook herself mentally and pulled her gaze to the DP. Dammit, ogling Matt *again*? "Let's try it with the natural light. Looks less like a TV set. Maybe move Her Highness's chair closer to the bay window."

"You're the boss." Much as Jamal would have, the cameraman hoisted a shoulder in resignation that he couldn't control the light as he obviously preferred.

She'd spoken to her injured friend that morning. He was healing, as was Vivian, thank God, but she still wished they were here. She was so hyped up before a shoot, they kept her calm. These new guys seemed as anxious as she was, maybe more.

Her cell phone vibrated in her pocket and she tapped

it open. Not a familiar number but the same area code as the federal prison. Her chest tightened.

What could Dad want? He never phoned before evening.

"Five minutes, people." She walked to the empty anteroom to take the call. Sarika's admin was inside with her boss and the others. She'd have privacy here. No need to walk any farther.

Chewing her cheek, she punched a key. "Dad?"

"Hello, Ms. Parker," an unfamiliar male voice said. "This is Associate Warden Thomason at Allenwood. I'm afraid I have some bad news."

Chapter Six

AS SHE LEFT to take her call, Matt caught her pleated brow and tight shoulders.

He could come up with several possibilities—funding problems, her injured friends, the network. Definitely not the rebels. If they tried to recruit her, she might not tell him, but she'd tell Sarika. She wouldn't cooperate with them, but he had to prove it to DARK, dammit.

He kept an eye on her through the doorway as he moved the princess's chair and helped Kelmen adjust the lighting to accommodate the daylight streaming from the balcony. Her expression became more agitated as she listened to the caller.

If he was alone, he could listen via his cell, using the app he'd placed in hers. So far all he'd heard was Thai take-out orders and girl chats with Sari. Today's call was something else, something serious. Too many people around for him to tune in.

Sarika took her seat in front of the bay window. She sent Matt a questioning look. He shook his head.

"Hey, dude." Kelmen mopped his brow with a lens paper. "Time is money. Where is she?"

"I'll get her." Matt wove through the maze of cables, cases, and tripods. He left the office, now a makeshift sound stage, followed by Traynor, Ingel, and his admin on their way out. He closed the office door behind him.

In the anteroom, he found Nadia seated on one of the chairs. Bent over in distress, she blew her nose into a tissue.

"Everyone's ready for the interview. What's wrong?"

She dabbed at teary eyes. "That was one of the wardens at Allenwood. My dad's been hurt. He's in the hospital." A sob shook her and she drew a deep breath.

Film shoot be damned. Matt knelt before her and placed his hands on her knees. "What happened?"

"Three inmates surrounded him in the dining hall this morning. There was a fight, and one of them stabbed him before guards intervened. 'Shanked' him, the warden said." Her voice caught.

"Will he be all right?"

"He lost a lot of blood, is in critical condition but improving. The warden wouldn't say he was out of danger." The anguish in her eyes faded as hot anger licked in. Pushing him aside, she surged to her feet. "As if you really cared."

Her pain sliced into him. He stood, but didn't reach for her. Helpless to comfort her, he fisted his hands at his sides. "I do care. I'm sorry he was hurt."

A deafening boom blew the office door off its hinges.

The blast threw Matt forward. He fell to the carpet, taking a wild-eyed Nadia with him.

Pulse racing and blood rushing in his ears, he covered her with his body.

Heat and debris roared over them.

Something popped and hissed.

Black smoke streamed from the princess's office.

Matt pushed up onto his elbows. He brushed

splintered wood and scraps of blood-covered paper from his shoulders. Around them lay results of the explosion—shards of wood and metal, a bloody embassy ID tag and other, more grisly evidence of violent death.

Bile rose in his throat and he willed it down. His heart hammered against his rib cage. Places on his back stung like the devil. He shook off the pain. "Are you hurt?"

Nadia shook her head, but a cut marred her right cheek. Blood dripped onto her jacket, which had a torn sleeve. She looked dazed, her eyes dark with distress. "What happened?"

"Bomb." The crackling sound from the other room meant fire. Fear propelled him upward. He grabbed her hands and helped her up. "You have to get out of here. To safety."

Lurching to her feet, she seemed to shake away her fog. Tears pooled in her eyes and she coughed from the smoke. "But Sari's in there. I have to go to her."

"No. Get help. I'll see about the princess."

Alarms shrieked. Footfalls pounded down the corridor. Over the noise and pandemonium sirens wailed.

Nadia took a stumbling step toward the burning office. He wrapped an arm around her shoulders to stop her.

"No, it's too dangerous," he rasped out, the smoke choking him. Maybe Sarika was alive. God, he hoped so.

He picked his way through the smoke and debris. Sunlight rendered garish camera parts and shredded upholstery strewn with body parts. Where the bay window had been, only a jagged gap and Sarika's overturned chair remained.

How could there be any survivors?

A sharp-clawed beast ripped through him, prodding him to howl and rage. He'd failed to find the traitor, failed to keep the princess safe, failed… again. He forced a deep breath. Clamped down on himself. This wasn't the fuck about him. He had to get Nadia out of here.

When he emerged from the horror, she rushed to him. "Sari?"

"The fire department and Security are coming. We need to get out of their way."

Fumes and heat billowed around them as the fire gathered force. His uncovered eye stung from the acrid stench. He didn't want to contemplate what might be burning. Nadia kept looking back but allowed him to drag her into the corridor.

Chaos reigned as clerical workers and dignitaries swarmed from their offices toward the front stairs and safety on Massachusetts Avenue.

"Stop, Matt, please," Nadia pleaded, pulling him aside into an alcove. "Tell me. Sari, the others?"

What could he say to her? He couldn't utter the words to tell her their friend was dead, her body shattered with the others, or blown out the window, to—

Tears stung his throat. He shook his head.

Modena Security raced toward the office with fire extinguishers. Three others followed, the Security chief among them—pistols drawn.

"There they are!" one shouted. He aimed his weapon at Matt and Nadia.

"Halt!" yelled another. Without waiting for compliance, the man raised his pistol. Fired a shot high, a warning. The bullet cracked into the plaster molding above Matt's head.

He was about to step out, hands raised, but Renzo's barked command froze him.

"Shoot them!"

Matt's pulse stuttered. What the hell! He pressed Nadia behind him with one arm. Somehow they were suspected of being the bombers.

The fire extinguishers accomplished little. Black clouds of smoke filled the corridor. Probably blinded the guards temporarily. Certainly slowed them. Ruined their aim.

He had to get Nadia out of there. Fast. Take advantage of the smoke screen. "When I give the signal, run like hell toward the service stairs in the rear."

"Why are they—"

"No time for questions. I know you don't trust me for much but trust me on this."

He hoped her lack of response meant agreement.

A group of five or six weeping women, more office staff, ran past them down the hall. They clustered around the guards, wailing and clutching at them.

Now that their pursuers were temporarily blocked, he and Nadia had to move. "Now!" Adrenaline spiking, he pulled her with him to race away through the noise and confusion.

Behind him, a gravelly voice yelled. "There they go!"

Crack.

The shot slammed into the wall inches from Nadia's head. She let out a small scream and sprinted ahead.

He swung around, searching for an alternate escape route. He pushed open the door to the stairwell. The pneumatic hinge would close the door slowly. Enough of a ruse. He hoped. He tugged Nadia along the hall and into the ladies' room.

He tucked her behind him against the wall while they waited. He felt her fear and shock like palpable vibrations in the air. He shoved down the same emotions. Put himself in the zone so he could function.

"Stay quiet and pray they think we took the stairs."

She gripped his shoulder with tense fingers, as if clawing her way out of a pit. She whispered, "Why are they shooting at *us*?"

It was a wide-open tiled room with sinks on one side and stalls on the other. Nowhere to hide. Then he spotted the mop bucket outside a closet.

"They'll look in the johns but not in here if I can work it right." He opened the closet door. Rolls of toilet paper and paper towels filled shelving on one side, but they could squeeze into the other and straddle the jugs of cleaning solution.

Nadia entered the small, dark space meekly enough. Her cheek continued to seep blood. Soot smeared her skin, ashen from the horrific shock.

He pulled the wheeled bucket toward the door as he closed it. The bucket clanked into the wooden door and stopped. His lungs pumped like bellows, and against his back, Nadia panted. "We have to calm our breathing," he whispered, "so they don't hear us."

Chapter Seven

NADIA BARELY HEARD Matt's words over the thundering of her heart. If she hadn't been pressed between the back wall and him, she couldn't have stayed on her feet. The bomb… the destruction… gunshots fired at them and… *Sarika!* How could she be— Nadia couldn't let herself think the word. Pain filled her chest, and her eyes burned with hot tears. She started to gasp, but Matt's warning registered. She took deep breaths and willed her heart to slow.

The restroom door swished open, followed by heavy footfalls. More than one person, Security searching for them. Praying Matt was right about their hiding place, she lowered her forehead against his warm, solid, reassuring back. Even the musk of his sweat reassured her.

Clanks and other noises, more footsteps as they searched the stalls. Then, "*Personne ici.*" No one here. How she remembered her French at this point was a miracle.

Another barked, "*Allons, à l'escalier.*" Let's go, to the stairs.

"*Ah, non, les autres a cherché là-bas.*"

A moment later, the two or maybe three guards slammed out of the restroom. The clicking of their shoe soles grew fainter as they trotted away.

She gulped in air, and thoughts spun in her head,

disjointed, jumbled. For a moment, she couldn't move.

Light sliced through the door opening as Matt pushed it open. "Stay put." His whisper grated like fine-textured sandpaper. Before she could react to ask what he was doing, he'd stepped around the mop bucket and crossed to the exit.

He peered out for barely a second and returned. "We have to move fast. They didn't take the stairs, so we will."

When she just stared at him, his gaze shifted from concerned to hard. He grabbed her hand and tugged. "Nadia! Let's go. You can fall apart later."

His words woke her like a splash of cold water. Fall apart? No, not her. She didn't fall apart when her mom died. She didn't fall apart when her father was charged and convicted on a guilty plea. And she wouldn't now. She straightened from her huddled stance and took off with him. She had to trust Matt's skills and experience. He knew better than she did how to get them out of here. And maybe out of this whole mess.

With alarms ringing in their ears and the smell of smoke drifting through the hall, they raced the short distance to the red exit sign. When they slipped into the stairwell, he said, "Go all the way to the basement," as he took off.

This was the third floor, so a long way down with no cover, no hiding place. "What if someone—"

"Keep going. Let me handle it." The footfalls and squeaks of his rubber soles echoed as he raced ahead of her.

Throat tight, she stared at the four stark-white walls of the vertical tunnel. She was alone. If guards—or anyone—showed up, she'd make an easy target. She wasted no more time and headed down at a fast clip. Second floor. First floor. Only one to go.

Nearing the next landing, she was breathing hard, and in spite of regular jogging and weight training, her legs were rubbery. Maybe it was shock and fear—

Thumping resounded below her. *"Fuck!"*

At the outcry, her pulse leaped. She slipped and grabbed the metal railing, but saw no guards, only Matt. He'd fallen and was tumbling down the last flight. He curled in on himself, tucking in his arms and protecting his head.

She winced at the thud of his body as his knees and arms and back struck the cement treads and the metal edges. She raced downward. How badly was he injured? What if he couldn't get up? He was a solid six feet. Pressed against him in the closet, she'd felt those hard muscles. How could she move him?

Reaching the bottom, she found him still, his visible eye closed. But panting as hard as she was, thank God. She knelt beside him. "Matt, where are you hurt?"

He hauled in deep breaths and lifted himself up on one elbow. He held up a hand in a *wait* signal.

She detected no voices, no sounds of doors or footsteps, only the stillness of this emergency stairwell. Maybe everyone had evacuated out front onto Mass Ave and forgot about them in the chaos. Not likely. For some strange reason, Security must think they were the bombers.

In a moment, Matt sat up and stretched his limbs, taking stock of the damage. "Lost focus and misjudged the distance. Missed a fucking step. Don't think anything's broken." He ripped off the patch, which had slid off to one side, and stuffed it in his jeans pocket.

Ah, the eye damage was the likely culprit. Depth perception. When she'd seen him before without the patch, he replaced it quickly. Now she could see that the lines above and below the patch weren't separate scars, but one continuous, jagged track. Puckered flesh on the eyelid marked where it had been struck. Other than that, the eye looked perfectly normal. She tried and failed to imagine how he must've felt to learn the vision loss might be permanent. Fifty-fifty, he'd told her, but his optimistic tone had sounded forced. He was probably terrified he'd lose the so-called freedom he'd told her five years ago that he needed in his life.

Now wasn't the time for advice on covering his eye with the offending patch. He was already beating himself up, so sympathy would only embarrass him. She pushed to her feet, digging for matter-of-fact. "Can you get up?"

He said nothing, only grasped the railing and pulled himself up. No bruises were visible, but no doubt black and blue marks would be blooming damned soon.

He dug in his front jeans pocket and pulled out his phone. "Looks intact." He stuffed it back in his pocket. "Take the battery out of your phone, so they can't trace us that way."

She knew that from the news and thriller novels, but wouldn't have thought of it. She removed her battery and put both phone and battery in her pants pockets. "What about yours?"

"Encrypted and secure, like all official communications," he said. "Only DARK can track me."

"The guards in the ladies' room said others had searched this stairwell, but I suspect someone might check again soon." Dammit, her voice was shaky.

"Forgot you knew French." He took a tentative step

and nearly went down again. His eyebrows drew together and sweat beaded on his forehead. "Must've wrenched my right knee when I hit the deck." A wry grin twisted his mouth. "Never thought I'd have to say this, but I'll have to lean on you."

"Wasn't on *my* bucket list." She wrapped an arm around his middle as he looped his right arm around her shoulders.

He hobbled a sort of hop-step and shuffle forward, and she pushed open the door. He peered out. "Nobody in sight. Head off to the left."

Nadia had never been in this rear part of the basement, far from the production company room and the employee dining hall. "You know where we are?"

"DARK had the building plans, and I did a little exploring." He indicated a shadowed corner and urged her forward as he hop-step-shuffled toward it.

An inset wooden door led them outside to an alley lined with metal trash cans and bigger bins on wheels. Her sneaker soles squelched on something, and she wrinkled her nose at the odors of rotting food and who knew what else. Late afternoon sunlight barely filtered into the narrow passage. A chain-link fence blocked one end.

"What now?" Nadia glanced toward the other end, which led to a street where cars whizzed by and people hurried along staring at their phones.

Leaving her support, Matt hop-shuffled to one bin. "I locked the exit door, but help me move this trash bin over."

She looked up and down the alley while pressing a hand to her jittery stomach. She then pushed with what strength she had left. Small metal wheels protested, the shriek jacking up her pulse again, but the heavy metal container rolled over to seal the door. She kicked the wheel locks into place.

"Better ditch your jacket in one of the others," he said as they headed toward the street end of the alley.

She looked down at herself. Yeah, sooty and torn and red. A trifecta. She might as well wave at Security and yell, "Shoot me." She retrieved a few things from the blazer pockets before slipping it off. She tossed it into the next bin.

The temperature was dropping as sunset neared, and she shivered. "The eye patch would've been as easy to spot. Is that why you took it off?"

"Sure. I don't need it anyway." Before she could react to that intriguing statement, he touched her cheek. "Cut doesn't look too bad, but it'll probably bruise. You got a tissue to wipe off the soot?"

She pulled one from a pocket and let him dab at her cheeks. The warmth of his fingers through the thin paper and the gentleness of his touch made her want to curl into him. Bad timing. Worse idea. "Okay now?"

He nodded and turned around. "I got a few cuts on my back. How about my shirt? Blood, soot?"

"Some slits in the fabric, maybe blood too. The shirt's so dark, nothing is really obvious." She hadn't noticed the tears in the dark closet when she'd been pressed against him. She reached out tentatively, but drew her hand back without touching. "Does it hurt?"

"Not much." He shrugged and put his arm around her, as ready to get going as she was. "Not like my damn knee."

She resumed her support and they headed for the street.

"This neighborhood's too upscale to have a sleazy corner bar, but there's a wine bar a couple blocks over where we can hang out until I can get DARK to pick us up." He'd been watching his footing, but as they reached the sidewalk, he turned toward her. "You okay?"

She nodded. "Peachy. You're the walking wounded. Can you make it the two blocks?"

"Moving around, I feel better. Just look at me with love in your eyes, honey."

She wrinkled her nose and did her best. As they strolled down the street, their arms around each other— in a manner of speaking—his body heat eased her chill. A few people smiled at the lovers, but most paid no attention and went about their business. Nadia noted Matt's labored breathing and that he made an effort not to lean on her too heavily. By now his knee was probably puffing up.

Their slow progress made the trek seem interminable. When she spotted a lighted sign reading Ambassador Wine Bar, she sagged with relief. The sidewalk tables were full of happy-hour patrons sampling the establishment's vintages and snacks. Matt led the way into the darkened interior, then to a glass-topped corner table. He sank onto a chair facing the street.

A guy in ripped jeans and a T-shirt whose design blended with the tattoos on his scrawny arms hustled over and took their order for coffees. Probably frowned on in a bar where wine labels covered the walls.

"Won't they search places like this?" She took the chair beside Matt.

"Yeah, but not yet. An embassy is sovereign territory, so the ambassador has to invite outside help.

55

Confusion and grief will delay an investigation. So we have a little time before the D.C. cops and the Feds start a search for us."

"How long do you think?" Her worried glance swept the entrance.

"Long enough to drink our coffee." He took his wallet from his back jeans pocket. "I'll get DARK to pick us up, but that could take time. In the meantime we need cash and some other stuff. An ATM and shops, a drugstore too, are down the street. Can you manage that while I stay here?" He handed her a debit card and recited the PIN.

When he finished listing the supplies they'd need, she turned over the card and frowned. "This belongs to a David Martinez."

"My alter ego when I need an alias." His lips curved, but it was a grim smile. "Spy, remember?"

Lights flashing, a white D.C. cruiser jerked to a stop at the curb.

Chapter Eight

THE WINE BAR'S outdoor patrons shaded their eyes against the light bar's strobe-like glare. Matt blinked and blinked again, furiously. Right eye closed, he looked down at the floor, up again in the direction of the light bar. What the—

"Oh, God, what do we do?"

At Nadia's hushed question, Matt pulled himself together. He squeezed the slim hand gripping his forearm. "Chill. It's not about us. Not yet. It's been less than an hour since the bombing." He could add that even if the officer was checking for them, he'd simply haul them in and DARK would spring them. But she might not take it as comforting as he would. "I'm going to have my coffee, and I suggest you do the same."

The tattooed server brought their order and the check and beat it back to the kitchen. Maybe the guy had cause to be leery of cops.

She sucked in a breath and picked up her mug with both hands.

A couple of minutes later, the cruiser took off again, siren screaming. Nadia relaxed against his side. Collapsed was more accurate. He'd take her nearness, the soft press of her breast against his arm, her scent, whatever the reason. Still, he needed to get them both out of here so he could think. And report in.

When she'd inhaled some caffeine and seemed

ready for the errands, he gave her directions and checked her on the PIN. Good to go. Nadia stood and started to walk away, but then turned back as if reluctant.

He winked at her. "Hey, a little shopping trip. What could go wrong?"

She rolled her eyes but then made her way outside.

He waited until she'd gone out of sight, and then covered his right eye again. He turned his head, sweeping his gaze over the tables, the mirrored wall, the entrance. His pulse tap-danced. He swallowed, hard. Yes! He could see! Not much, but more than shadows. Fuzzy shapes and more light. He couldn't yet rely on vision in that eye, but for the first time the possibility of real healing wasn't just a pipe dream. Wearing the patch for most of every day, he hadn't realized.

After a long drink of the hot java—holding the cup with both shaking hands—he took out his phone. He speed dialed his contact officer.

"About time. What the hell's going on?" Stratton barked into Matt's ear.

"I missed you too." He lowered his voice. "Hangin' out trying not to get shot. Could've used the cavalry in that clusterfuck." When silence was the only reply, he brought the other man up to speed. "We booked it down the street and are lying low. So what's going on at the Modena embassy?"

"I'm getting zip from the bugs you planted because most people evacuated. Video surveillance shows personnel still standing around outside. Modena Security faced off with D.C. Metropolitan PD uniforms for a while, but now there seems to be a truce, and cops have cordoned off the street. Fire trucks, ambulances still there. I saw a couple FBI higher-ups go in, so the ambassador must've requested U.S. help. I expect Secret Service to show up next. So far it's only the cops scrambling to look for you and Parker."

Matt hung his head. "Any word on the princess?"

"Nothing yet."

"You have any idea why Modena Security thinks Nadia and I are to blame?"

"No idea. I'm waiting for a call back from a Feeb buddy of mine. How'd the two of you avoid being confetti?

Matt explained why they'd left the princess's office. "Can you get me anything about Isaac Parker's being shanked?" For Nadia, but also because the attack might be connected to the bombing.

"I'll see what I can do. But I can say you were right to be suspicious of the substitute film crew. Phony IDs, and they spoofed the website so theirs looked like the real deal. They must've worked in the business, so we're digging for more."

"They knew filming, for damn sure. They could've smuggled in explosives in the equipment, maybe C-4." Matt shook his head. "If they brought in the bomb, did they intend to hide it in Sarika's office and then leave? Or did it go off by accident? If they didn't smuggle it in, the smoke and mirrors to get the gig make no sense. They're definitely involved. Still, the bomb could've been brought in by any of the others who left before the interview was to start." He listed the names.

"Roger. Will look deeper," Stratton said.

"So when can you send someone to bring us in?"

The long pause didn't lighten Matt's mood. "Cardona probably planned the bombing and his inside partner carried it out, whether or not the film crew did the smuggling or were just scoping out the place. DARK knows you're not guilty, and nobody knows about the undercover op except the princess and us. Let the Feebs and Modena Security work on the bombing angle. The CO wants to set up a trap for the rebel leader."

Crap. This op's control officer was Ken Ritter. Always one for grandstanding while others did the grunt work. "You're not bringing us in, are you?"

"Not the way you mean." Stratton cleared his throat. "Let someone know where to pick you both up. Ritter wants to question Parker, find out if she was involved."

The coffee he'd drunk turned to acid in his stomach. His hand tightened around the phone. "Nadia's no more guilty than I am."

"Not my call, man. Just follow orders."

"Like hell! Ritter always thought she'd conspired with her old man. He would twist her words, make her look guilty, like he almost did five years ago. You know it and I know it. Princess Sarika was—*is*—her friend. She'd *never* harm her. She's been through enough."

"You sure you're thinking straight about this woman, Leoni?" Stratton's words were measured and clipped. "Didn't the director order you to keep an eye on her?"

"Fuck this. I'll be in touch."

Matt disconnected. He jabbed a finger at the edge of the phone back. Fucking fingers wouldn't cooperate. Fucking phone slipped and fell on the floor. He bent over to retrieve it, but twisted his knee. The pain, like knives filleting the joint, made him suck in a breath. Still puffing, he bent more carefully and hooked the phone. He sure as hell wasn't going to let Ritter railroad Nadia. And for no fucking reason. Finally the phone back popped off, and he removed the battery.

Nadia had nothing to do with the rebels, the bombing—none of it. He rubbed his knee, now swollen so much his pants leg was tight. Aw, hell. Ritter might hang her out to dry, and being on the street with Matt and his gimpy knee might put her in the crosshairs. A tossup.

But no telling what could happen if Ritter grilled her and turned her loose without protection. Matt wouldn't put it past him. Modena Security might scoop her up. If Renzo didn't shoot first, his people wouldn't be gentle about interrogating her. Or Cardona's rebels might grab her, set her up her as the scapegoat. Matt couldn't help Sarika, but he sure as hell could protect Nadia.

He stared out at the street, willing her to return so they could get out of here. A woman wearing a nubby white pullover, a short skirt and low-heeled shoes ambled his way. She carried a cane and a large plastic shopping bag. With every step, the bag swished against her long, sexy legs.

In spite of everything, he smiled. He pushed to his feet and tossed money on the table. He had an idea of their next move, provided he could still hobble. They had to hurry before the night closed in.

****

An hour later, Nadia was adding the finishing touches to her task. The lamppost, too far away from their bench, cast only feeble light on her subject.

During their nerve-racking walk from the wine bar, everyone they'd passed seemed to look at them with suspicion. Only her imagination, but still… Here in Rock Creek Park the traffic fumes were left behind. Only muted traffic noises penetrated the trees. The quiet and the green earthen smells eased the cold hollowness inside her. She drew a deep breath and surveyed her handiwork. Almost finished.

Matt's eyes remained closed as she applied another layer of foundation to the scars above and below his eye, avoiding the eyelid. Touching him like this, smoothing on the makeup with her fingertips, was way too intimate. Was the nearness affecting him too? Possibly. He might've been asleep except for his tight grip on the edge of the park bench. Or his tension might be due to pain. His swollen right knee must be throbbing. Damn, bad word choice.

The makeup should hide most of the scars, and anyone searching for them wouldn't look twice at a man without a black eye patch. She tilted her head. If he didn't need it, why wear the patch? Because slashing red scars weren't sexy but an eye patch was?

Or hiding behind it because he feared he might not regain vision in that eye? Or because it made him look dangerous rather than damaged? Hell, she was finding it harder and harder to resent the man.

Especially after the way he took charge and saved her. After the gentleness of his touch when he'd doctored the cut on her cheek and pressed on a small bandage. And after she'd had her hands on his back—his muscular, naked back. Only to put antiseptic and bandages on his cuts, but oh my…

She shook off the heat sparking in her belly and backed up. As she wiped her fingers on a tissue, she nibbled on her lower lip. The park trail, both ways, was mercifully empty. The paths and grounds were growing too dark for walkers and joggers. Too dark for Matt and her too. They had to find somewhere he could put up his leg and apply ice and the stretchy binding she'd purchased.

"Finished making me look all girly?"

She jumped. Nope, he hadn't been asleep. "Don't know about girly, but you're ready for the camera." She dropped the makeup into the shopping bag and pulled out a gray hooded sweatshirt and a faded Orioles baseball cap. "For you."

Putting on the garments, he eyed what else she held. "A fedora? Really?"

"Wait." She wound her hair on top her head and secured it with a scrunchie. "See, the hat hides my long hair. Voilà, my disguise."

"Not bad." He pushed stiffly to his feet. "Anyone would think you made spy movies instead of documentaries. You've done great here, buying thrift-shop clothes so they don't look too new."

"*Consignment* shop," she corrected. "Remember, it's an upscale neigh—" A siren's wail choked off her reply and shot her pulse into the stratosphere. Her chin trembled. In the fading daylight doing their damn disguises, she'd let herself feel secure, but now the shadows closed in. Once the siren had faded, she blinked furiously. "I… I… the bomb, Sari…" The words scraped across her heart. She lifted her hands, and then let them fall to her sides.

He pulled her into his arms and kissed her forehead. "Easy. About Sarika, everything, we'll talk. Soon, but not here. Come on. We're just a hot babe in a fedora and a gimpy guy with a cane." He backed away so fast she might've imagined the warmth of his embrace. Was he worried she'd slug him? But then his big hand enfolded her shaking one. "What d'you say we get out of here and flag down a cab?"

His question confused her. "Why a cab? Didn't you say you'd have DARK pick us up?"

Chapter Nine

MATT'S MIND RACED. He would come clean
with her, but not until they were tucked in a hotel room
farther away from the Kalorama neighborhood. "I called
my DARK contact while you were shopping. Kelman
and Herbert were phonies. They were involved in the
bombing somehow, and my contact's working on it. But
he can't send anyone for us yet. We're on our own for
now. I got this, Nadia." He crossed mental fingers she
would continue to trust him.

Her expression unreadable, she studied his face for
a moment. "A cab you said. To where?"

He allowed himself an inner sigh of relief. It could
be another day or more before he could come up with
something, anything—like a trap for Cardona. Damn
Ritter for mistrusting Nadia! He gestured at his worn
sweatshirt. "We'll need better clothes than you found in
that shop, enough for a couple nights in a hotel. And I
need some stuff from a locker I keep."

"A locker? Why do you keep things in a locker?"

"Spy, remember?" He twirled an imaginary
mustache. "In case an op goes sour, I can disappear fast."

She slanted him a skeptical look, but when he
headed toward the street, so did she.

Two cabs passed them by on busy Connecticut
Avenue, but they caught the next as it was depositing a
group of Asians near the Chinese Embassy. He

announced their destination as the Greek restaurant on Irving. Nadia's eyebrows winged upward. Paying them no attention, the Nigerian driver negotiated the traffic, still rush-hour heavy at nearly seven. Matt figured no one had followed them from the park, but turning around to check would look like what it was. Not worth giving the guy a reason to remember them beyond Matt's limp.

After paying the cabbie at the restaurant, he checked the traffic behind the taxi. Satisfied, he pulled Nadia over to the posted menu.

"Looks good," she said. "I like moussaka, but I doubt hunger pangs are what brought you here."

He could quip that he was hungry for her, which was always the truth, but he turned around and urged her toward the street. When she started to speak, he shook his head and, when there was a break in the traffic, hurried her across—not as fast as he wanted because of the damn knee. Closed-circuit cameras poked out from ceilings and over shop doors, but his and Nadia's altered appearances shouldn't trigger recognition from any watchers.

Inside, a uniformed D.C. Metro cop, hand on his utility belt, ambled toward them down the wide corridor as he talked on his phone. Nadia gripped Matt's arm, and he planted a kiss on her temple, lingering long enough to breathe her in. That lilac scent—soap or shampoo—and the light tang of nervous sweat.

The cop walked on past them.

In one of the department stores, they found everything they needed. Khakis and a green dress shirt for him, a blue skirt and matching pullover for her and rain jackets for them both because the taxi's radio had mentioned fog and rain.

He left Nadia and the shopping bags in the Columbia Bar and Grill—perfect, no cc cameras—and collected his go bag from his sports club locker. It contained essentials for being on the run—including his personal sidearm. The 9mm fit his hand better than the agency's .40 caliber weapon. The pack also held a fresh pack of gum. He stuck a piece in his mouth and forced interest on his face as the gym trainer bent both his ears about some fucking new health regimen guaranteed to build muscle and male stamina. Matt figured that made the company ripe for lawsuits. The trainer claimed it would heal Matt's sprained knee. Finally, after lying that he'd sprained his knee playing pick-up basketball, he got away with the bag, equipped with backpack straps. Carrying it on his back made it a hell of a lot easier to manage while using a cane.

He hustled back, ignoring the throbbing with every step. Had he left her too long? What if she'd bolted? But when he skidded into the bar, she was working her way through a goblet of white wine and a bowl of chips.

Tamping down his hard breathing, he stuck the gum in a paper napkin and snagged a couple of chips. He noted the shadows beneath her eyes. She had to be exhausted from fear and worry, but she never quit on him. Bold and creative and gutsy. "You okay?"

She wagged her shoulders and took a drink.

Okay but shaky. Hell, so was he. The place was about half full. Women with shopping bags, suits—male and female—with briefcases, maybe some students from Howard, and a few hardcore drinkers bent over shots and beers at the bar. A guy alone at a table gave Nadia a leering once-over, but at Matt's stinkeye, he decided to study his drink instead.

Damn straight. "We should eat. Then we'll get a hotel room."

That right eyebrow arched again. She crunched into a chip. "*A* hotel room?"

"Absolutely. I'm not leaving you unprotected."

At her mutinous expression, he couldn't help but grin, ready to counter any objections. But the server, an older woman in black pants and the bar's logo T-shirt, arrived and took their orders. "I'll bring that beer right over, hon."

Nadia was staring at a couple standing by the bar. Then she shrugged. "I had a déjà vu moment there but whatever memory it almost triggered is gone." She picked up her wine and finished the last drops. "You're right about the hotel room and security. Plus it's your money. I do appreciate that. I'll repay you."

"Not necessary. I have money socked away. Never have time to spend it." He glanced up as the server returned with his beer and another white wine. "Thanks." He dropped his DARK cell in his pack and withdrew a battery and another phone, one of several he'd installed with blocking software. He put in the battery and booted up.

Nadia's gaze was lowered to her wine glass, the corners of her mouth turned down. When she looked up, her eyes were bleak. "The film crew. I hired them. If they did this, the explosion, it's my fault. I... killed—"

"Never!" She shouldn't even give thought to the idea or voice to the words. Shit, she was heaping guilt on top of her grief. He glanced around. Nobody turned their way. People were either focused on their booze or staring at the local news broadcast, images of a car pile-up on one of the city's arteries. He lowered his voice anyway.

"Don't even think it. This disaster is all on me. I should've done more, and faster."

"I hired them, didn't I? I should've known something was odd when they contacted me about the job. Kelmen said he'd seen my search on the clearing-house website. But I was desperate."

"Hey, even DARK's background check okayed them at first."

Her frown said she wasn't convinced. "Kelmen was always hurrying, but why did he care? Their contract with me was for two weeks, with a provision for more days if we fell behind. He and Herbert both seemed extra nervous this morning. I assumed they were dumbstruck by the princess's presence." Her chin wobbled, but she straightened and recovered.

Her ability to pull herself together impressed him. She was tough. "When I left to find you, he said, 'Time is money.' I'd heard him say it before, figured he used it to keep shoots moving. Maybe this time he meant more. Maybe the bomb was on a timer." He tipped up his beer and pictured the scene. The two men had never been out of his sight. He had nothing. No idea unless… "Or did they intend to leave it behind so they could trigger it later?"

She nodded. "When they'd have been safely away. But how'd they hide it? We were right there. If they left any equipment behind when the shoot ended, I'd have noticed. Or else they had nothing to do with the bomb. If you and I had been in that office—" She shook her head, as if refusing the logical conclusion. "Matt, you said that DARK cleared them 'at first.' Do you know more than you've told me?"

Shit, no reason not to share—about the phony crew

at least. He explained about the spoofed website. "For damn sure they were involved. Why and how they got caught up in the blast is the question. I should've gotten the dirt on them earlier. Pushed DARK to dig deeper. Thought I had time."

"Look at this, Tanisha," one of the drinkers at the bar yelled. "She's alive!"

"Told you, Bert." The server sashayed over and wagged her finger at the bartender. "I win the bet."

The sound on the news feed was muted, but on the big TV screen, wording scrolled across a recent video of Sarika and the First Lady in the Rose Garden. His breath caught in his throat. A glance at Nadia—eyes wide, hand to her lips—told him she saw it too.

The typing did a snail's crawl, and after a dozen eons, revealed, "…be killed in a bomb blast. But Modena's Crown Princess Sarika is reported to be in critical condition at Walter Reed National Military Medical Center."

"Oh, Matt," Nadia whispered, tears glistening in her eyes.

He gripped her shaking hand with both of his. *She's not dead. Thank you, God.* "Don't say anything. Be cool." As if *he* could, but he managed to keep his expression impassive.

She blinked back her tears and blew into a napkin.

The server bustled over and set down their plates. "Burger for the gent and crab cakes for the lady." She beamed them a wide smile and winked. "Special evening for you two lovebirds?"

He threaded his fingers with Nadia's. "I'm working on it."

She coughed as if she'd nearly choked. But her lips

curved in a grin, a little tight and forced, but brimming with hope. "Special is right."

Her fingers untwined from his, and he had no choice but to let her break the connection.

Nadia clasped her hands in her lap, savoring the warm tingle from Matt's touch. Finally, she picked up her fork. She didn't think she could eat a bite, but his rumbled words and sexy smirk had made her laugh in spite of everything. Enough to find her voice. And her appetite.

And now she had hope. Sarika was alive! Critical but alive. Walter Reed treated soldiers with terrible war wounds, so she'd receive the best possible care. She'd be all right. She would. She had to be.

The Maryland crab cakes were surprisingly delicious. Who knew a mall bar would have a decent chef? Well, a *cook* was more like it. But still. While they ate, she watched Matt fiddle with his new phone, the one from his pack. He told her he was searching for a hotel. He shook his head and stowed his phone when the server brought their check.

They changed into their new clothes in the mall restrooms and stuffed everything else into his pack. Rides on two Metro lines delivered them to Union Station. They entered the main hall and stood to one side near the Mass Ave exit. Aromas of grilling burgers wafted from a nearby restaurant. Travelers, commuters, and shoppers streamed past them.

She bit her lower lip, checking everyone who passed and every cop in uniform while he did another search on his phone. No one even looked their way. Voices and shoe heels echoed off the barrel-vaulted ceiling, gleaming white with gold leaf touches. She remembered reading somewhere the station had been refurbished since the earthquake in 2011. She feigned a bored-girlfriend look, and made herself stare upward at the few dozen statuary on the balconies. Why Roman soldiers with shields? Probably to go with the exterior's classical design, but still bizarre. And naked.

"Lots of hotels in Georgetown." Matt's voice, low and confiding and sexy, drat the man, brought her back from her musings. "And far enough away from Kalorama. We don't want a small boutique hotel. Too easy for staff to pay attention to us." A frown skewing his scars, he continued scrolling.

"When I was here during Dad's trial, I stayed at the Prospect Hotel. Pretty big, a tourist hotel with lots of families and couples. Pricey though." Too high for her budget, but she'd needed to be in town, not in the suburbs. "Too long ago for anyone there to remember me."

"Sounds good." He kept his head down over the screen and scrolled. "Got it." With a few more clicks, he was able to book a room.

They made their way outside, through the portico and a pair of enormous marble pillars onto a broad sidewalk. Nadia shivered in the cooler air and was grateful she wore the new jacket. She'd expected darkness would hide them by now, but safety lighting made the night as bright as day.

Two men and two women loitered near the taxi line. They seemed to be studying faces and glancing at their phones.

Her heart sank into her belly. "Matt."

Chapter Ten

"I SEE THEM. This way. Slowly, casually." Matt took her arm and turned right, away from the taxis.

They strolled around the next pillar and back inside.

"Okay, new plan," he said. "They're looking for a couple. We'll split up and take separate cabs."

Nadia shook her head. Her whole body quaked with fear and exhaustion. Because of his throbbing knee, Matt had to be worse off, but he kept going, like that battery bunny. The image nearly made her smile, except her lips wouldn't move.

She dragged in a breath and straightened her shoulders. "It's not Modena Security. They won't shoot us. It's DARK or the FBI. Why not let them take us in? We'd be safe and maybe I could go to the hospital and visit Sarika."

"I know you want to see her. So do I, but it's not possible right away. Those people out there aren't DARK or I'd know them. They're FBI. Even in jeans and windbreakers, they look like they should be wearing black suits. I'll explain later why turning ourselves over to them is a bad idea." He set down his pack and cupped her shoulders. "Being on the run is stressful. Hell, more than stressful, it's terrifying. You're a trouper, Nadia."

His strength and the heat of his hands seeped through the jacket, easing her nerves and making her want to lean into him and feel his arms around her. And not just because he was protecting her and organizing their "getaway." She felt every millimeter of contact, and a flicker, a quiver low in her belly. No way, not him, even if she needed him now. She went for flippant. "Thank you for that. What's that fabulous new plan? A magic carpet? Or asking Scotty to beam us up?"

He tugged her closer, but quickly released her, as if not realizing what he'd done. "Think of it as being in your own documentary."

"Feels more like a Dan Brown thriller."

He grinned. "Close. Here's what I'd like you to do."

At least he'd asked and not ordered. When she nodded, he withdrew a second phone from a pouch on his pack. "I'm putting my new number on speed dial for you."

She gaped at the pack. "How many of those phones do you have?"

"Dunno. Maybe a dozen burners and more SIM cards," he said as he programmed the phone for her.

He handed it to her along with more cash. Still pondering his foresight and—what should she call it, spycraft?—she tucked both in her small, new handbag. She concentrated as he told her to take a cab to the Ritz-Carlton.

When she frowned in confusion, he held up a hand. "Separate, remember. Hang out in the lobby and wait for my call. I don't think you'll have any problems, but if anybody followed you or is watching you or—" he stopped, his mouth tight, probably hated scaring her further "—the FBI or anybody has you, answer the call with 'sweetheart.'"

She frowned and her chin wobbled, but she sucked back her trepidation. "You're going to the Prospect Hotel and call me at the Ritz-Carleton?" Of course. His knee must be killing him, especially with the extra weight of that pack. He was limping more.

"That's it. I hate sending you out alone, but—" He gave his knee a middle-finger salute, as much complaining as a macho spy could allow himself. "Can you do this?" He studied her, his expression hot and piercing.

"Absolutely." She could, even if her insides quivered like jelly in an earthquake. She turned away to leave him.

Matt's arm shot out and his hand clasped hers.

She gasped as he reeled her into his arms. His warm mouth covered hers and the light rasp of his scruff on her skin gave her goosebumps. The touch of his tongue urging her lips to open made her insides clench, and she opened to his hunger. His kiss was tender and claiming and tasted of spearmint. She had no idea how long the embrace continued, only that she didn't want it to end. A guttural sound from his throat resonated within her.

He lowered his arms and stepped back. "Go."

She nodded, her pulse rioting, her knees wobbly as a new foal's. Calm, steady, she told herself as she forced herself to walk away.

****

Matt watched her from the shadows as she walked across the wide apron and to the taxi queue.

He drew deep breaths and ordered his body to stand down. He'd heard the desperation in her voice, seen it in her gaze. She'd needed support, and grabbing her, holding her, the kiss, whatever, was supposed to be merely that. Like sending her into battle. He winced. Definitely not that. He'd wanted to kiss her. Hell, it might have been his only chance. A sneak attack. *Shit, stop with the war analogies!*

The Feebs paid her no attention. Except for the one guy who checked out her legs. Five minutes later, the yellow cab she entered pulled away, and he could breathe again.

He waited another ten minutes before shouldering his pack. He hobbled toward the cab line. At least six people ahead of him, not counting two families with piles of luggage. They'd need a vehicle bigger than a sedan.

One of the male FBI agents turned toward him. Shit, they'd met once or twice at coordination meetings. Smithers, maybe Smitts… or something. Would the guy remember him? He kept walking, kept looking straight ahead. No need to exaggerate the limp. The swelling was taking care of that.

The guy cocked his head, squinted. Could be the glare of the pole lights. Or not.

Matt kept walking, kept his gaze on his destination except for covert glances at the agent.

The man looked down at his phone, likely at Matt's official DARK photo, the new one with scars and eye patch. Looked up again. At the awkward gait, at the backpack, at his face. Smithers/Smitts dropped the phone in his pocket and headed toward him.

Matt kept moving, kept his expression neutral. Hoped sweat hadn't washed away the makeup covering the scars.

The agent passed him and continued out of sight, either behind the pillars or into the terminal.

Figuring the guy could still be watching him, Matt resisted the urge to look back. The other Feebs appeared focused on the crowd in general. Didn't look at their phones. Didn't look his way.

He joined the taxi queue and waited the forty-seven centuries it took for him to climb into a cab.

****

At the Prospect Hotel, Matt shrugged off his pack and tossed it on the floor, along with the cane. He crossed to the window and twitched aside the sheer curtain. If the desk clerk had cared at all, he probably thought Matt requested the street side to save money, but if any government entity located them, they'd more likely set up surveillance on this side than along the side overlooking the Potomac. Outside now, some pedestrians with briefcases, couples who might be headed out to dinner, no obvious Feebs. Nobody at all loitering unless you counted the valet-parking attendants.

A snail could've beat his cab through the traffic from the train station. Even with the painful balloon that used to be his knee, he could've walked the distance faster. So unless Nadia's cabbie drove a flying car, she might've barely made it to the Ritz-Carlton by now. He didn't want to risk calling her if she was still en route. He didn't like it, but he'd give her a few minutes.

After filling the purchased ice bag with the hotel's cubes, he settled on one of the queen beds. He propped the bag on his knee and let the chill seep in through his jeans. "Deflate, damn you, deflate."

He dialed Stratton's cell number. Fifty-fifty whether his friend would answer, but Matt wanted more info before divulging anything more to Nadia.

"Yo, who is this?"

The rumble of a Harley-Davidson assured him that Stratton was out of the office and couldn't easily do a trace. "Chill, Cole. It's me."

"You have any idea what firestorm you started, Leoni?" the other man barked. "Going off the reservation, taking a suspect with you—"

"Whoa, fucking whoa! She's a *suspect* now?"

Grumbled sigh in his ear. "More a person of interest. Ritter kept me at HQ until late. His head may explode before this is over. Do you realize what you've done? The risks you're taking?"

Matt stared at the phone screen. The risks he was taking? No shit. He could lose— He wouldn't think about that. This was about protecting Nadia. Ritter would interrogate her, terrify her, and then have her locked away somewhere, and Matt could do zip. She'd been through enough. He'd gotten her out of danger and he'd keep her out. "I know the risks." The words scraped his throat like broken glass.

"Where the hell are you?"

He resisted replying with the childhood taunt *for me to know and you to find out*. "In the wind. Any new developments?"

The bike's engine cut off as Stratton gave in to having a conversation. Sounds of other vehicle engines firing up echoed. He was probably in the parking building. "This afternoon, the Modena Security office received an anonymous phone tip that the film crew were tied in with the rebels and had smuggled in an explosive. Security guys were heading to the princess's office when the bomb went off."

"The reason they shot at us," Matt said as much to himself as to the other man. "Any chance of a trace?"

Stratton snorted. "Non-working number, burner phone. But the admin who took the call said the male voice had an accent that could've been from Modena. She was pretty shaken up, so who knows."

"Cardona or a minion."

"Possibly a way to divert attention from their spy inside the embassy."

"Or to set us up to take the fall when the bomb went off," Matt said. Without the call to Nadia, they'd have all been killed, phony crew included. That part didn't fit. They needed more intel. "Anything new about the princess's condition or Nadia's father?"

"I got nothing, only info about the three dead, what's left of them. But I can check if you want. So about Parker, why is she afraid to come in?"

"I'm not talking to you about her, not unless Ritter changes his mind about interrogating her."

"Only *questioning*. Come on, it's not the third degree. What could he do?" Stratton's tone was even, but pressing for more discussion. Why?

Light tapping sounds over the phone, on a tablet or another phone. Matt sat up straight, the move knocking away the ice bag. He poised his thumb over the red receiver icon. "You ready to trap Cardona?"

"Ritter and the AD are working on a plan, but—"

"I'll see what I can come up with on my end. I'll contact you when I have something." He disconnected before the other man could alert somebody in DARK to trace Matt's phone's location. Triangulation was the best they could do, but he'd rather not give them the chance.

Dammit to hell. And now he was late calling Nadia. Waiting for the connection, he held his breath.

"Oh, thank God," she said. "Are you okay?"

He exhaled, and his shoulders relaxed. She was safe, alone, but ready to jump out of her skin. And she was worried about *him*? "All set. You sure you had no problems?"

"Only traffic. There's a snazzy company party here, so no one's paying any attention to me. I'm gawking at the evening clothes while pretending to do email on this phone."

"Well played, Mata Hari." A small laugh from her, the deep chuckle he hadn't heard this time around, reassured him and turned him on. "You probably won't need this info, but just in case. We're registered as Mr. and Mrs. Paul Malik." He spelled the last name.

"And do *I* get a first name?" She huffed, but with humor, not irritation. Or fear. Good.

"Amy." His high school girlfriend, but he'd stay mum on that. He gave her the room number and a knock code. "Walk through the lobby to the elevators without stopping."

"I remember the layout. I'm leaving now."

"Take M Street, not the smaller side streets. Safer with all the night life there. Don't stop anywhere or talk to anybody. Come straight here."

"Yes, Mom." She disconnected before he could dredge up a laugh.

And now he waited. Again. Surveillance duty had taught him patience and alertness. So had the instances when he had to go deep and hide out. But this was different. This was Nadia. He was alert all right. And sweating. He held the ice bag against his forehead.

Chapter Eleven

TWENTY AGONIZING MINUTES after Matt's call, Nadia stepped onto the seventh floor of the Prospect Hotel. As the doors swooshed closed behind her, she jumped, her heart drumming. For no good reason. She'd been the only person in the elevator. Drawing a deep breath, she wiped her clammy hands inside her jacket pockets.

As instructed, she'd made no stops from the Ritz-Carlton and walked briskly, hoping she appeared relaxed as she headed for a dinner date. Or in her case, a rendezvous in a hotel room. No one looked at her twice, and no one seemed to have followed her.

Not that the ever-present fear had vanished. All her nerves were afire. If only this were over. If only she could talk to Dad. If only she knew more about Sari. Her fingers cramped and she flexed her clenched hands. Maybe Matt had good news.

The polished brass sign on the wall ahead indicated the direction of the room, and she turned left. The hall was empty except for a couple of room-service trays. She stood at the door, just stood, couldn't move just yet. Would he kiss her again? Did she want him to?

She closed her eyes, replaying their embrace at the station. His kiss had been both ardent and tender, melting her against his hard body, so she could barely stand. The solid feel of his body against her sent thrills to body parts too long neglected. In a sensual haze, she'd somehow found her way to the taxi stand. She shook away the tingling sensations conjured by the memory. And the fantasy.

Wait, what was the coded knock? One and then two or was it two and then one? She closed her eyes and concentrated. Two and then one.

Matt yanked open the door immediately. He pulled her into his arms and kicked the door closed. No lip-lock this time. He only examined her as if to make sure she was whole, and then placed a chaste but warm kiss on her forehead, just enough to banish the chill inside her. She clung to him, savoring the rasp of his jaw against her skin, the press of his solid chest against her tight nipples. She ached for him to put his mouth—that wide, sensual mouth with the fuller bottom lip—lower. And lower, everywhere. But she stepped back, away. She couldn't give in to her treacherous body, to wanting to escape the madness with him.

She couldn't betray her father with Matt.

He didn't seem to notice her hesitation. He gripped her shoulders. "You're good? Nobody followed you?" As if trying to see inside her, he peered hard into her eyes.

She lifted one shoulder in an elaborate shrug. "I made sure I wasn't followed." She sidestepped him and checked out the room. Bathroom was spacious, plenty of towels, good lighting. Desk with all the technology connections, poster-size framed photographs of the city rather than generic prints.

For some reason, she felt compelled to describe her safety measures. "I stopped twice to check the reflection in store windows."

He nodded, lowering himself to one of the beds.

"Other people got off the elevator at lower floors, but the thought occurred to me that someone—an FBI agent, a Modena rebel?—could've noted the number of my floor. So I pushed a higher floor and continued up before coming back down. Alone. No one else got in the elevator."

"I have no reason to think either of us was followed from the train station. What you did verifies that. Good technique, subtle and efficient." His amused tone suggested she'd been amateurish using methods gleaned from movies—which was true—but maybe he was just happy she made it safely.

"Thank you, oh Master Spy." She crossed the room, past the beds, two queens as he'd promised. Matt had placed all her purchases and her other clothes on the second bed, as if to make clear his good intentions. She tamped down the fillip of disappointment. "Nice room, bigger than I had back when. And they've remodeled."

"Glad you approve." He glanced around as if seeing the décor for the first time.

And perhaps that was true. The ice bag drooped over his knee. He'd been busy with the ice and waiting to phone her. "Let me refill that for you. The bag looks a little flat, but not the knee. How's it feel?"

"Ibuprofen's helping. So's the ice."

"And the back?" She started to reach out, but linked her fingers together instead. Lifting his shirt and putting her hand on his naked back, and him on a bed? Significant parts of her grew hot just thinking about it, dammit. "Should I check it? Put more antiseptic on the cuts? All that... stuff that hit you could cause infection."

He sent her a cocky grin. "Nah, feels fine."

A sigh wove through her, but was it relief or disappointment? "Okay, then. But you'll need the bandages changed sometime." They were likely in for the night. So before bed. *Bed. Two beds, remember.*

She turned her back on him and crossed to the bathroom, where she emptied water from the bag into the sink. Breaking eye contact seemed to douse the electric awareness fizzing through her.

After refilling the bag from the ice bucket, she handed it to him. "So how long do we have to wait for DARK to scoop us up? I need to check on my dad, and I'd like to know more about Sari's condition." Her eyes burned. Seeking control, she bit her lower lip.

His expression darkened, and he squirmed around before settling as if for a long chat. Or for an uncomfortable one.

Her stomach tightened. Did he have bad news? Was it Sarika? *Oh, Sari…*

Before she could ask, he said, "I know you're worried, but I have nothing new on Sari, but I do have some things to tell you. In a minute. First, my pack there on the floor, would you get out the bottle and pour me some over ice?"

She gaped at him, at his stony expression, a long few seconds. When he didn't elaborate, she dug into the pack through clothing and… a pistol, which shouldn't have surprised her. Actually, knowing he was armed reassured her. The bottle was nestled in a sweatshirt. "A fifth of Jack Daniels? You've been carrying that all this time?"

"Had the cabbie stop at a liquor store on the way here." His little-boy grin triggered warmth low in her belly.

"But you're hurt. Are you—"

"Sure? Damn sure. The drink?" He jerked a thumb toward the ice bucket. "You'd go against the wishes of an injured man?"

She glared at him, and then shrugged off her ire. He wouldn't be driving. She poured his drink and one for herself diluted with a little water.

She handed over his glass and sat on the edge of his bed. "So, DARK?"

"I can't tell you everything, you understand." She raised an eyebrow to convey her skepticism. "My contact confirmed that the dead in the blast were Kelmen and Herbert and the princess's admin."

Her throat stung with the shame that she'd forgotten to even ask about the other person in the room along with her crew and Sari. "Pascale was a lovely person. She left a husband and a teenage daughter. I'll contact her family as soon as I can. Anything on my dad?"

"My contact had nothing new about Sarika or your dad's injury. I'm sorry about that, but you understand why you can't call the prison." There had to be a way, somehow. All she could do was nod as he went on. "DARK learned that that Modena Security received an anonymous tip just before the bombing." He gave her a highlights reel of the call—the timing, the circumstances.

She shuddered. "One of those burner phones, like we're using. No wonder they were shooting at us."

"DARK is staying under the radar on the investigation because nobody's to know about my undercover role. The mission's control officer wants to set up a trap for Sandor Cardona, who's made it into the country. Reports indicate he may even be in D.C."

Nadia studied his expression. No longer stony, but

carefully bland, eyelashes at half-mast—and sexy, dammit—back to his sloth-like persona. During film school and for her own films, she'd interviewed enough politicians, executives, and activists to know that everyone hid something. Behind those sleepy brown eyes Matt was hiding something. "Why aren't you telling me about DARK bringing us in?"

He set his glass on the bedside table and clasped her free hand. "Because it sucks, that's why. Ken Ritter is my control officer. You must remember him."

Her brows snapped together and she jerked with such vehemence, liquid sloshed out of her glass and onto her skirt. "That bastard! How could I forget? He yelled at me, stalked around me, scared the crap out of me, all while I was frantic to talk to Dad, to find out what was really going on. He treated me as if *I* was the one who sold secret plans to terrorists."

"Bastard, yes." Matt kept possession of her hand. "When Ritter gets hold of something, he doesn't let go, even when he's wrong. More than once he's gone overboard and come up sputtering, but other times he's popped up crowing with triumph. I suspect he goes for recognition rather than the agency's goals."

"What does this have to do with now?" At Matt's down-turned mouth, she regretted asking.

"When I called in, I was told somebody would pick us up, so I could help plan the trap and so Ritter could question you." That hit her so hard, he might've slapped her. She opened her mouth to say, well, she didn't know what, but Matt shook his head. "Take a healthy slug of your drink and hear me out."

She did as he said, savored the burn in her throat, and willed her pulse to settle. Hand shaking, she set the glass beside his. "O-okay, so?"

"Ritter still doesn't trust you, thinks you could've been bribed by the rebels. I don't trust *him* to treat you fairly. So we're on our own for now. We need rest. While DARK works on a plan, we're safe here, off the street. And while I work on who could help us, somebody who won't betray me... or *you*."

Taking all that in without running screaming from the room was a struggle. She jumped up and paced a circle while her brain spun faster than a computer hard drive.

After a few deep breaths, her temper cooled, and so did her head. Something didn't jibe. Even if DARK loaned Matt to the Modena royals to find the rebel traitor, there was more to the matter. Correction, more to the mission.

She returned to her seat on Matt's bed, where she could watch his expression. Closely. "If you're supposed to report to a control officer—" she couldn't help a curl of her lip at the thought of Ritter calling the shots "— DARK is more involved than you're telling me. Why does a U.S. anti-terrorism agency care about a rebellion on little ol' Modena?"

He scraped a hand through his hair and downed the last of his drink. "I'm already up to my neck in shit, so I might as well spill. A Yamari extremist group called New Dawn is dumping cash and weapons into Sandor Cardona's cause to eliminate the royalty and take over the government. Their goal is controlling the former U.S. naval base on the island."

She clutched at the bedspread, a whirlwind tunneling her vision. In deep, measured tones, Matt continued to explain. A slow-mo montage of horrific possibilities reeled across her mind's eye, *terrorists… Russians… base of operations*. Terrorists controlling a port in the Mediterranean? Unthinkable.

"The king discounts the terrorist threat, so DARK is operating in secret. Our goal is to roll up Cardona and eliminate any possibility of a foothold by New Dawn. To date we're not even on the fucking playing board, let alone back to square one. It's like wrestling smoke." He slapped his empty glass onto the table so hard she jumped.

"The naval base. I ran across the history of it in my research on Modena. I had no idea…" Her throat was so tight, the words came out barely above a whisper. She forced down a swallow and wished she'd refilled her glass. "And now DARK—and you—are scrambling for a plan to trap Cardona."

He nodded. "And now you know what's at stake."

"Not only that. I'm in the way, keeping you from contributing to the search for Cardona, for concocting a plan, for—"

His big, capable hands grasped her shoulders. "No!" Apparently thinking he'd hurt her, he relaxed his grip and his palms circled warm comfort. "Our being on the run is keeping Cardona and whoever is helping him on edge. That works in our favor—or the agency's favor."

She studied him, searching his dark gaze for dissembling. Seeing nothing but honest concern and maybe something more, she eased away and stood. "I need to think. And I need a shower."

"For what it's worth," he said in a soft tone, "I'm sorry I had to lay all that on you. If only a shower could wash away trouble."

"Exactly."

"One more thing. Sarika doesn't know about the terrorist connection. Her father didn't want to worry her."

"Because he doesn't believe in the threat." She shook her head at the unreasonableness of that. And the tragedy.

She left him with his ice and Jack. Her small bag of toiletries in hand, she grabbed the long sleep tee she'd purchased. As she dashed into the bathroom, she caught sizzle in his heavy-lidded gaze. Matching heat streaked through her body.

Turning up the water as hot as she could tolerate, she dropped her head and let the powerful pulsing spray loosen her tight shoulder and neck muscles. She washed with the hotel's gel and shampoo, labeled Herbal Serenity. If only. At least the crisp aroma of lavender and the tang of lemongrass were cleansing away the grime of the explosion and the sweat of their run to safety—and her fear.

Rinsing her hair, she let the tears flow. For Sari, who might be healing or sinking. For her father, who— How bad were his injuries? Would he survive? Why had those men attacked him? More tears for the future of her dreams, now well and truly trashed. She'd worked so hard to achieve even a small measure of acceptance and validity in the documentary arena. And now this. If not for Matt, she might be in detention somewhere in a DARK or FBI basement. If Modena Security didn't shoot her. If not for Matt…

She opened her eyes and turned off the water. Matt had disabled his secure DARK phone, cutting himself off from his team. And the two of them were using burners. No batteries in those either. He was hiding her.

Protecting her. Sure, he'd said being on the run had an advantage, but did he just make that up on the spot to ease her anxiety?

Matt was defying orders by not delivering her for questioning. Risking his job, the career he loved. And more.

Didn't Feds have to take some sort of oath? Just how much *was* he risking—and why?

For *her*? What else wasn't he telling her?

She shivered, but not from the water cooling on her skin.

Chapter Twelve

THE BATHROOM DOOR opened, and Nadia padded out barefoot in a cloud of scented steam that triggered a memory of his mother's garden, not lilacs, but herbs he couldn't name. He pictured his mom kneeling among her plants, weeding, gathering herbs she'd use in lasagna or chicken primavera. Basil maybe, or something lemony, like now. Mom would've liked Nadia.

The memory faded as he registered faint purple bruising surrounding the cut on her cheek. At least she didn't seem bothered by the injury.

Even with her face bare of makeup and her hair wound in a towel, she was so beautiful he went hard in a nanosecond. The sleep shirt reached mid-thigh, giving him an eyeful of toned legs. On the shirt, a cartoon cat winked, and a speech balloon in a comic font read "Naughty Dreams." Damn straight.

He raised his uninjured knee to hide his condition, which knocked the ice bag off his right. Clearing the scratchiness from his throat, he pushed up higher on the pillows. "Feel better?"

"Definitely." She sat on the side of her bed facing him and swept off the towel. She scrubbed at her hair with it. "And you, how's the knee?"

"Better. Swelling's down." But only on the knee. Having her sitting there drying her hair like they were damn college roommates was somehow more intimate than their almost sex of five years ago. He wanted her so bad, he ached. At this rate, he'd need ice on more than his knee.

"And the eye? You're rubbing at the scars and still no eye patch. Do you want me to get it?" She moved as if to go for his pack.

Didn't realize. He lowered his hand. "I don't need the patch." At her raised brows, he heaved a sigh. Why not? "Haven't needed it since they took off the bandages."

A puzzled expression creased her forehead. "I see." She winced. "Sorry for the choice of words."

But she probably didn't see. He wasn't sure he did. "The patch made it easier for other people. My eye, the scars looked damned ugly at first. And then…" Why did he keep wearing it after that? He couldn't think of a good reason. He shrugged and let a grin hide his ambivalence.

"Can you tell me how the injury happened? Or is that classified?"

"I can tell you most of what happened. It didn't get wide coverage."

"I remember something about it. Not much," she said. "But generally we don't know about all the attacks security agencies *prevent*."

"Sad but true." He held up his glass and widened his grin. "My Jack needs refreshing."

Instead of the disapproval he expected, she draped the towel over one shoulder and picked up both glasses. With her hair loose and messy, she looked sexy as hell.

When she returned, her hair was combed and she'd poured them both new drinks. "The mission?"

"This one involved a cell of New Dawn."

92

"The same ones cozying up to Cardona?"

"The very same. A nice bunch of assholes. They were led by a Belgian national named Pierre Orland, a petty criminal calling himself Saleh. They planned to detonate a bomb outside the European Union Council building."

Her eyes widened. "On the Rue de la Loi, right in the center of Brussels."

"Lots of traffic, lots of people, not far from the metro station that ISIS bombed."

"I remember. Another attack at the airport a few years ago, men with bombs in suitcases." She swallowed a big gulp before setting her glass on the night stand and gazing at him, head tilted.

After a slug of liquid courage, he took a deep breath. "Intel didn't pick up on those in time to stop them, but our resources have improved. Members of the council would've been arriving for a big meeting when Saleh planned to set off their bomb. A suitcase filled with explosives, nails and other projectiles. We located the terrorists two days before the scheduled attack. Cleared the corner building except for their flat. We calculated they hadn't had time to put the explosives and parts together. We deployed around the building. Eurocorps agents went inside. They broke in, got three men down on the floor. Saleh wasn't one of them."

He liked that she didn't interrupt, chatter away. She nodded encouragement and watched him, the same intensity and need to know in her pretty green eyes as during her video interviews. Her legs were crossed, and her foot swung back and forth, drawing his gaze. Not looking her in the eyes made it easier to recount what happened next.

"I spotted Saleh climb out a basement window and hustle to the sidewalk. My team and I went after him. When he saw us, he reached for a cord on his backpack. I fired my weapon. As he dropped, he pulled the cord. The bomb detonated." Matt didn't remember anything afterward until he woke up in the hospital. He met her focused gaze and gestured at his scars. "That's how I got this. My body armor saved me from worse."

Her forehead crinkled, and her eyes softened with sympathy. "So they'd had time to create the bomb after all."

"The backpack held a smaller device. Their fail-safe, we decided. In the flat, agents found the components for a much bigger bomb. We were lucky."

After recounting the experience so many times in official reports, he could recite it, at least the short version, without his gut churning and his chest seizing up so his lungs hurt. Even that took him back.

He could smell his sweat and feel the press and weight of the Kevlar wrapping his body. He could hear, muffled through his headset, the noises of struggle and metal cuffs from the conspirators' flat. He could see the fury in Saleh's eyes when Matt raised his MP5 and his triumphant grin the millisecond before he detonated the bomb. Damn, Matt wished he could've seen the dumb fuck's face when he realized there were no forty virgins waiting for him. Not even one. And no Paradise.

"I see," she said, unease edging her words. "Were you the only one hurt? No one except the terrorist was killed?"

He should've known that as inquisitive as she was, she'd press him for more details. "I woke up in the hospital with the news that two members of my DARK team were killed. Kirby Nashota and Sara Malik. They'd run too close to the damn terrorist. Their body armor wasn't enough to shield them." The photos of their bloodied and mangled bodies on the paving stones were burned into his brain. "We all carried nine mil submachine guns. If I'd raised mine faster...."

A sympathetic murmur came from Nadia. "I'm so sorry. Something you never forget, just as we won't forget what happened this morning. And then you learned about the damage to your eye."

Thank God her next words had veered back to him. He'd shared all he could stand about his dead friends. He lifted his gaze from the melting ice in his drink. "Hey, but my vision's coming back. I can see shadows and faint light."

Her concerned gaze turned speculative. She tilted her head. "Odd, but I don't hear much enthusiasm in your voice."

He'd said enough about his vision and the deaths. "What about your film after this morning? Delays, a new crew, what? Here's to healing."

He held out her glass. When she took it, he clinked his against it.

Nadia's heart set up a clatter. The question had come out of the blue, but she should've expected he'd ask. She drew a deep breath. "What happens? In a word, ruination."

"Nadia, this will all be cleared up in a few days. You won't be blamed, you'll see. And you have insurance, right?" Matt's voice as well as his gaze was warm and sympathetic. Could he really understand?

"Yes, of course. Equipment can be replaced." She traced lines in the glass's condensation. "But I needed this project on the Modena royals. The king needed it and was being very generous. All that's up in the air now. The contract guaranteed double the money if we wrapped early. It would've meant—" she might as well tell him "—enough to start another appeal for my dad. Enough for me to move to more meaningful films. All that may be gone now. And I was looking forward to seeing my mom's homeland. I wanted to go when we were in college, and Sari even invited me, but her family never agreed. I never learned why." She took a sip of her drink and set it away again.

"So you have family on Modena?"

"I don't know for sure. Mom never would say more than that she didn't get along with her family. Dad's the only family I have left. He's seventy-three, his health isn't the best, and now he's injured. I need to get him out of that prison." Her breath hitched, and she bit her lower lip on that last note of hopelessness.

"Don't give up." Matt set down his glass and collected her shaking hands. "I'll do what I can to help. When this whole mess ends, the king will still want the documentary. Be grateful you have your dad. More than I have."

His words, his sort-of promise soothed her. "I've told you more than I usually share about my family and my dreams. We have this stolen time together, so we might as well understand each other better. Tell me about your parents—before."

His shoulders wagged in a barely-there shrug of acquiescence. "Sure. My dad was on the job, a Boston police detective. Mom was a police social worker, involved in crisis intervention and mediation, lots of work with domestic violence and kids. That's how they met. My dad's folks celebrated when he found an Italian girl to marry." He looked away, memories curving his lips, as if he could see his parents. Then his expression darkened.

"Tell me what you most remember about them." It was the kind of question she often asked in interviews, but this time she felt invested in a personal, not professional, way.

His gaze seemed to turn inward before he met hers. "Dad gave me my first baseball bat and mitt. He never lost patience with me when I struggled to hit even his fat pitches. And I like to look back at when Dad took me to Red Sox games. We'd go once a season."

"And your mom?" She longed to tuck back a lock of hair that straggled onto his forehead, but she didn't want him to release her hands.

"Even as busy as she was, she had a garden and was a great cook. Mom was a people person. The house was always full of neighbors and friends—hers and dad's and mine. She always had cookies for my buddies and me." He turned his head, and his jaw worked. "In the afternoon she baked for a charity auction, and then, that evening—" His grip on her hands tightened almost painfully.

"You don't have to tell me the rest."

"Yeah, I do. You didn't believe me before, so I want you to know it all."

"Matt—"

He opened his hands and let hers go. Immediately she missed the warmth and assurance.

"Dad was lead detective on a money-laundering and drug case. They had evidence that would put away the top gang members. He and Mom went out to celebrate their wedding anniversary. As they were leaving the restaurant—Antonio's on the South End, their favorite—they were shot from a black car that sped away. Both of them. They died on the sidewalk." His shoulders drooped, and he shook his head.

Murder. The tragedy of it squeezed her chest. "I'm so sorry. Did… did the police catch them?"

"That's the only good thing. Surveillance cameras caught the license number and the face of the shooter. He spilled on his bosses. So in addition to the other charges, three men went down for murder."

"And you went into foster care? No aunts, uncles, grandparents?"

"Grandparents had passed. No one else. Funny, huh, a bare-bones Italian family? Money from the police fund and the folks' insurance gave me college money, and I joined the Boston PD after."

Murder had taken away his family, and foster "no-care" made him an outsider. Anger and resentment had blurred her understanding of how hard he worked, how dedicated he was. Now she got it, but did he? He wanted to make a difference, to contribute, but more than anything, he needed to belong.

"And then DARK," she said. "From one team of comrades to another. Fighting crime, corruption, and now terrorism. No matter what you've said about needing freedom and control over your life, I don't see that you have much of either. DARK is your family substitute, a group to belong to, but you go where they send you and do what they order."

"That's not how it is at all." He slugged down a hefty drink of Jack and turned away his gaze.

Denial, but she'd touched a nerve. No point in

poking the bear. He was a good man, doing what he thought was right, protecting her, and trying to figure out how to stop the Modena rebels even if it put him at risk. "Why are you doing this now? Risking your career to go on the run with me?"

There it was, that boyish grin that sparked her nerve endings. He rubbed the back of his neck. "Beats me." At the shock that must be on her face, he shook his head. "Not a time to joke, sorry. You got a raw deal from DARK before. I couldn't let that happen again. It looks like Cardona framed us for the bombing, and I can't be sure he wouldn't use you again, whether you're here or in DARK's hands. And... I do care about you." His expression was carefully neutral, but his faint color marked his cheeks.

Warmth suffused her belly. Care about her? What did that mean? And did she want him to care about her? She couldn't return the feeling, she couldn't. No matter how hard she tried not to care, she felt more than sexual attraction for him too. The few days of working with him had awakened all the old emotions that tangled up her mind and heated her body. And now he was risking everything to protect her.

She'd thought to allow herself only to trust him to keep her safe. But now.... "I trust you to know what you're doing," she said, "and I trust you to protect me. I care about you too, but I don't know if I can give you a pass on five years ago. My dad—" Her voice broke.

He pressed a finger to her lips. "Enough with the walks down memory lane. It's nothing but a mine field. It's late, time we turned in." He picked up his now-sloshing ice bag and stood. "Now I'm the one who needs a shower."

"The cuts on your back, you should have antibiotic cream and—"

"Don't worry about it. I'm fine. Just fine." The bathroom door closed quietly behind him. But the soft click hit her ears like a slam.

Chapter Thirteen

AT TWO IN the morning, mist and fog dimmed the view outside the Prospect Hotel. Matt could pick out nobody loitering nearby. A light rain fell on the nearly deserted street. A figure huddled in a slicker hurried past the entrance. An occasional car or delivery truck passed. That was all. Even squinting, he couldn't see much. An apt metaphor. He couldn't penetrate the shadows inside himself or out there either.

Instead of keeping watch and worrying, he should try to get some sleep. He'd need to be alert when they left the hotel. At least he'd finally figured out who might help them. *Might* being the key word.

A noise behind him jerked him around. His hand automatically went for his weapon, but of course it was in his pack. Nobody was in the room but them. He straightened, rolled his shoulders. There was the sound again.

It was Nadia. She whimpered and thrashed, tangled in the sheets. "No... no...." Then something unintelligible. She gasped, twisted as if to sit up, mumbled again.

She was okay. She'd wake up soon. Just a dream. Or should he go to her? He watched her for a few seconds. She continued to fret, in the throes of her nightmare. Leaving the curtains open, he crossed to her bedside in the semi-dark room. "Nadia?"

She rolled onto her back. Her long sleep shirt was all twisted, the V-neck askew, and the ambient light from the street highlighted a pale pink nipple. Heat spilled through him. He swallowed. The light glinted on her wet cheeks.

Tears. Dammit. For Sarika, her father, herself? Or vague weirdness, the aftermath of that horror show this morning? He sat on the bed. Reached out, pulled back his hand. Shit. She was still thrashing, nearly sobbing. He couldn't let this continue.

He took a deep breath and placed both hands on her quaking shoulders. "Nadia, wake up. Nadia, it's Matt."

A pained gasp escaped her as her green eyes opened and she jerked upright. "Wha—"

"Easy, easy. It's just me. You were having a nightmare. You're okay." He didn't want to scare her further, so he let his hands fall away.

"Oh, it was awful." She flung her arms around his neck and held on for dear life. "Flames and smoke all around. I could see Sari… and my dad, but the flames…." She sobbed against his shoulder.

He wrapped his arms around her slender quaking body and breathed her in, the scent of her hair, her skin, sweet and spicy, like her. Her breasts were pressed against his bare chest. His dick exulted into action, and he willed the growing arousal to subside. She was frightened and heartbroken, and for a while he could handle just holding her.

Her head lifted, and her beautiful liquid eyes met his. She kissed him. And kissed him. He couldn't ignore the feel of her lips, soft and plump. On autopilot, he tangled his tongue with hers and kissed her with a thoroughness that drove them both into a state of frenzy.

A lightning bolt of need shot down his spine. Her slender fingers brushed his neck, teasing the hairs at his nape and making him shiver. He touched his mouth to her jaw, licked the softer skin on her neck. Damn, he wanted to lick every inch of her. Murmurs hummed from her throat. And his. She was as turned on as he was. The realization swelled him to an ache that headed toward desperate.

He could barely think through the haze, but he must. He had the hots for a woman who hated his guts a few days ago, who didn't trust him, and who he was supposed to be spying on. Triple damn. She scooted closer, so close she had to feel the Louisville Slugger between his legs. He'd never forgotten her, had wanted this amazing woman for too long. So talented, so loyal, so beautiful. Maybe…

He eased her away a few inches, not ready to let go. If ever. Placed a hand on her uninjured cheek and tangled his fingers in the warm silk of her hair. "Nadia, honey, it's just the nightmare. It's not me you want."

Her eyes flashed. Even in the semi-dark, he recognized that look. "Don't you think I know what I want? I sure as hell know what *you* want." She proved it by reaching between them and grasping him through the thin cotton of his boxers. Engorged with need, his dick jerked in her hand. He groaned and sucked in a breath. "This isn't about undying love, Matteo Leoni. It's about tonight, a man and a woman and feeling alive. It's about sex. Just sex. "

He didn't speak. Hell, he had no argument against her faultless logic. Really? She wanted this—him, no strings, no recriminations, no tomorrow? Wasn't that all he wanted? Well, yeah, but why did hearing her say it bug him? And there was his mandate to spy on her. But everything had changed, hadn't it? He had to think. Fuck, at this point, with her in his arms and his little brain in her soft, warm hand, he could barely think at all.

He saw her sag. Her lips thinned. Shit, now she thought he was turning her down. In a strained voice, he said, "Honey, if it's just sex you want, I'm ready. More than ready. Hey, it's never *just* sex, well, for me. I mean. I thought you wouldn't trust me because of well, um, and I had to be sure. You know. Hell, I sound like an idiot."

She chuckled. Thank God it wasn't an all-out belly laugh. "You're forgiven. For the dithering, I mean. Understandable under the circumstances. Can we pick up where we left off?"

Before sliding her hand away, for emphasis, or maybe seduction, she gave him another squeeze, and he went to granite. Five years ago, he'd made himself hold back. No more. They were in this together, and he needed this as much as she did. It might be their only chance to be together. "Let's get you out of that shirt. I want to see more than one nipple."

Her brows rose. She looked down at herself and laughed. "Let's." She shimmied around, tugging the shirt from beneath her and then up and off.

"Beautiful. Perfect." As always, except now he could see more of her. Her breasts weren't big, but a generous handful, sweet as he remembered. She was trim and fit, but a wonder of curves. He bent and flicked his tongue over one nipple and then the other. Both peaked under his attentions.

And it was her turn to suck in a breath. "Matt."

He kissed her again and scooted off the bed. "Don't go anywhere."

"You're leaving me? *Now*?"

In an inner pocket of his pack he found what he needed. He returned to the bed, shucked his boxers and lay beside her. He wouldn't push, would let her set the pace. But jeez, he ached to be inside her. Now.

She tossed back the covers and browsed his shoulders and chest and on downward to his straining dick, her gaze zapping nerve endings in its path. She nodded toward the handful of foil packets he'd dumped on the bedside table. "Ambitious, aren't you?" Her husky voice betrayed her arousal.

"Honey, I've been waiting years to be horizontal with you. We might need more. I just hope I can hold out long enough to put one on."

"Oh, I do like a challenge." She hiked one sexy leg over his hip. The little circles she licked over his nipples made him groan. Her scent spiced with their mutual arousal teased his senses. One hand cruised over his shoulders and down his pecs. "You've been working out." Her other hand floated downward past his bellybutton to the part of him that strained upward. She stroked the vein, circled the tip until she coaxed out a pearl of moisture, and then closed soft fingers around him.

He jerked in her hand. "Boredom. Desk duty," he rasped out. His heart was racing. Enough talk. More action.

He covered her mouth with his, feeling the hot sweep of her tongue against his, intent and insistent. Pulling her closer, he slipped one hand between her legs—no panties to strip off, yes!—found the sensitive nub and gently massaged. She arched against him, her kiss hot and demanding, her sighs rising and falling. She was slick and wet, ready for him. Sweet. Liquid fire raced through his body, and he craved her with near pain. She was witty, smart, sexy, and brave. No other woman had ever affected him so, tangling up what his body wanted with his mind, his emotions… no, he wasn't going there.

He lay back and grabbed one of the packets. Struggled to rip it open with his teeth while keeping one hand on her smooth, soft skin.

"Here, let me." She opened the foil and rolled the condom on him one agonizing millimeter at a time.

High-voltage flashes scorched him. "You trying to kill me, Nadia?"

She laughed and opened her arms. "*La petite mort*, the little death, as the French call a climax. Let's find it together."

Their mouths met as he entered her, and every muscle in his body tightened, every cell celebrated. He stroked in and out of her delicious heat—his, hers, he didn't know—heat that burned his body from the inside out, heat he never wanted to leave, heat ripping up his spine in a wave and tightening his balls. He clenched his jaw. Dammit, he'd hold out, take them both all the way. And then she arched and cried out, her strong thighs clamping his hips as the pulsing took her, and he let his own release explode from him, sweeping him with such exhilaration he was left gasping for breath.

Long moments later, he rolled off her. After making use of a wad of tissues to clean up, he pulled up the covers and gathered her into his arms. "Go to sleep now. After that, no nightmares."

"You promise? We might need another round to make sure."

He smiled into the darkness. She was something. "Give me a few and I'll be up for it."

She walked her fingers down his belly and patted him. "How about now?"

Damned if he didn't twitch to life beneath her touch.

Chapter Fourteen

NADIA CLOSED THE bathroom door behind her and leaned against it. In the bedroom, snoring. Light, but steady. Matt was still asleep, although the gray light announced it was a little past dawn.

Matt. Last night was magical. Lovemaking with him was so spectacular, she still tingled. His enthusiasm knew no bounds, and he was playful, not just single-minded like some guys, aiming just for the climax. He relished in her taking the initiative, humming his pleasure as she threaded her fingers in his soft chest hair and kneaded the beautiful muscles there. She'd cupped his taut butt, hell, fondled his whole impressive body. Just thinking about their night started the pulsing within her.

As horrific as the situation was, she couldn't regret fate bringing them together. She accepted he'd been caught between duty and desire five years ago, but hadn't spied on her or used her. She'd told him she couldn't give him a pass on all that, but she would tell him she'd changed her mind. Especially now that she understood better what made him tick.

It was clear to her if not to him that he didn't feel he deserved to regain his vision. He blamed himself for the deaths of his teammates in that Brussels mission. The reason he hid behind the eye patch for so long. He'd still be hiding behind it if not for yesterday's explosion. And worse, losing the vision in his left eye could take him away from his only remaining family, his colleagues in DARK.

Despite that, hiding her, running with her counter to orders was the biggest risk of all. His career, his freedom, his life—all were at stake. No matter how he'd brushed that off.

So she didn't take lightly what she must do now. She hated deceiving him and hated the possibility of their being detected. Fear was a live thing in her belly, but she *had* to know.

The light on the hotel hair dryer casing allowed her to see well enough.

She slipped the battery into her phone, hers, not the burner, and turned it on. The prison's automatic system answered at the second ring, but it took several minutes before she reached someone she knew, someone who'd tell her anything. Her dad wasn't in the prison infirmary, but in the local hospital, thankfully no longer in intensive care. Armed with the hospital number, she eventually reached his room.

While the phone rang, she pressed her ear to the bathroom door. Only an occasional snort. As if cold fingers had brushed her neck, she shivered, praying that turning on her phone wouldn't invite danger.

"Hello?"

"Dad?"

"Aw, Nadie, honey. Thank God, I was so worried when I heard. Then I saw on TV… the bomb—" His voice broke.

At his weak voice and the pet name, her eyes burned. How like him to worry about her, when he was the one who'd been so injured. She'd tell him as little as possible about what was happening on her end. "Dad, I was outside the room, not hurt at all. I'm fine, but I'm worried about you."

"Oh, I'll be fine. I have more stitches than that rag doll you used to tote around, and I hurt like the very devil, but they tell me I'll heal."

She smiled. If he admitted he hurt, he was feeling better. "Can you tell me what happened?"

Silence, as if he was deciding how much to tell, or else gathering strength. She was about to speak, but he said, "It was three prisoners, convicted terrorists, not from Al Qaeda, like before, but some other group. Too many to keep track of these days, you know. It was the third time they'd approached me. I thought they'd given up."

"Given up on what? What did they want?" But she feared she knew.

"Honey, they wanted me to get you to help them, something with the Modena Embassy, maybe that bombing. I didn't want anything to do with it or them. Because I betrayed my country before, they thought I'd betray it again—and you. I regret what I did because in the end I lost the woman I loved anyway, and I will forever regret the pain my crime caused you, the setback to your promising career, the shame."

"Oh, Dad, you don't have to—"

"But I do. Let me get this out. The hurt and accusation in your eyes when you learned what I'd done and again when I was arrested cut me deeper than any knife these thugs could wield. I refused them three times. This time they didn't ask. They just jumped me."

She leaned against the wall and shook her head to rid herself of images of that attack. If he'd played along, or told the officials, or her, maybe the bombing wouldn't have happened, no one would've died and Sarika would be safe and whole. But Nadia knew why he told no one. He doubted they would give credence to the complaint of a traitor. Sadly, he was probably correct.

"And now, now have you told the authorities why you were attacked, what they wanted?"

"I have, but I don't know what good it will do."

She saw no point in going through his transgressions. Her mom's illness had been so expensive. Insurance had covered much of the chemo, the radiation and the surgeries, but the desperate searches for a miracle had not only painfully delayed the inevitable, but also depleted their finances. When Isaac Parker could obtain no more loans for experimental treatments in Mexico or China or for the next charlatan who offered hope, the terrorists had come calling on this illustrator of highly classified defense systems manuals.

Once she was no longer in danger, she'd see what she could do. Tears fell on her phone, and she swiped them away. "Dad, I'm so sorry."

"Yes, me too. More than I can express. Sorry about all of it. Now and back then. But I loved—" A cough racked him.

When the wheezing stopped, she gathered herself and said, "Dad, I just wanted to check on you. I'll let you rest now."

"No, stay. There's something I *have* to tell you. In case, well, just in case. I promised Irena."

The familiar pang of loss hit her, and she pressed a palm against her stomach. "Promised Mom what?"

Sounds of nose blowing and deep breathing came through the phone. "Nadie, I love you. I've loved you from the moment I felt you kick against Irena's belly. I burped you and hugged you when you first called me Dada and bandaged scraped knees and wiped tears. I did it all with the love of a father for his daughter. I'm your father in every way except by blood."

She could barely take in his flood of words. "W-what?"

"I'm not your birth father. Irena was pregnant when I met her."

The admission flash froze her insides. "Not my birth father?" Her knees quivered, and she sank onto the cool tile floor. "No, no, no."

****

Matt dropped his phone and the battery into his pack and slipped back into bed.

He ached to open that door and pull her into his arms. Not her real father, and she never knew. Never even suspected. And she had to deal with it now all by herself. Matt couldn't tell her he'd overheard. Tiger claws clamped his chest at that blatant lie. Hell, not overheard, he'd *spied* on her, exactly what she'd accused him of before. It would make no difference to her that it was under orders. Shit. He wouldn't sleep again, but he'd have to pretend once she'd pulled herself together enough to return to bed.

Somebody likely got a hit on her phone or his and would be searching the environs of the nearest cell tower. They'd have to leave this hotel and Georgetown. As soon as possible.

A while later, the bathroom door opened, and Nadia returned. On a muffled sniff, she snuggled against his back. For warmth? Or comfort? *Aw, honey.* Now they were both pretending to sleep.

When the traffic noises picked up below on M Street, he checked the bedside clock. Eight. He tossed off the sheet and padded to the window. Hey, barely any pain, and not much swelling. No sprain after all. No telling what they'd be up against today. He might need to move fast.

Covering his right eye with one hand, he allowed himself a grin at seeing clearer shapes, not just shadows. Hope, but not there yet. He uncovered the eye and checked the scene outside. Same as last night. A few pedestrians with umbrellas. Traffic moving along. No obvious surveillance.

"Nice view." She spoke from the bed.

The sound of her voice, although deeper than usual and sexy-rough, jolted heat through him. Bad timing. Keeping his naked backside to her, he willed his body to subside. She probably figured he'd chalk up her voice quality to sleep, not the aftermath of tears. "Should be the sun and not a moon."

She hooted a laugh. Good his bad joke could get that reaction. "Has the rain stopped?"

"You wish. A steady drizzle, mixed with fog and mist." He turned toward her.

A small smile curved her lips, but her eyes held the bleakness of her conversation with her father. If only they could talk about it. If only he could comfort her. But any comfort had to be couched in solving their shared predicament. Dammit, he hated lying to her!

Sitting in a puddle of sheet, she reached up to smooth her hair. The action lifted her bare breasts, the nipples erect in the air-conditioning. And now *he* was erect.

He climbed back into bed and took her in his arms.

"Hey, beautiful. Leave the hair alone. Sexy as hell."

"Thanks. You look pretty sexy yourself this morning." She ran the knuckles of one hand across his stubble.

They kissed until both were breathing hard. He wished like hell they could take the time, spend the whole day in bed. That would more than comfort them both.

He ended the kiss but kept his forehead against hers. "I'd love to pick up where we left off last night, but we should get moving. It's not safe to stay in the same place another day. We'll have breakfast and head out."

After she'd finished in the bathroom, he showered but skipped shaving, leaving the early-morning look, since it seemed to appeal to Nadia. She put the finishing touches on the scar-hiding makeup around his left eye. "Your knee must be better. You're not limping."

"Yeah. As long as I don't twist it much."

Two firm knocks sounded on the door.

Chapter Fifteen

A MALE VOICE on the other side of the door said, "Room service."

Last night, Matt had ordered breakfast for about this time. "Nobody's seen you yet. No reason to let a hotel employee be able to give your description. Wait in the bathroom while I get this."

As soon as she'd disappeared, he grabbed his 9mm and went to the door. He stood to one side. "Who is it?"

"Room service, sir," said the youthful male voice.

"What's on the tray?"

After a beat, metal clattered. "Um, one On-the Go breakfast, egg and cheese on an English muffin. And a banana." Another clatter as he lifted the other lid. "One Hearty Start. That's eggs—these are scrambled—with bacon and hash browns. Toast. Coffee and juice for two. Looks like grapefruit. Pink."

The waiter had nailed it. He sounded nervous but not scared. So no Feeb or worse asshole standing to the side, gun drawn.

Matt stashed the pistol behind his back and fished a ten out of his wallet. He opened the door. The freckle-faced kid looked barely old enough to shave. "Working your way through college?"

The guy nodded. His Adam's apple jumped. "And learning the menu so I can get a raise."

"You deserve one." Matt handed over the bill and

lifted the tray from the trolley. "I got this. Thanks for the delivery."

The kid's mouth was hanging open as the door swung shut. Matt leaned against it until it latched. "Coast is clear. Breakfast is served."

Brow crimped and fingers mangled together, she emerged from the bathroom.

"Only a waiter with higher ambitions. We're good." So far. He set the tray on the desk and arranged their breakfasts on the small window-side table.

"You do that like you've waited on a few tables yourself."

"Long time ago. In college." He waved her toward the table's one chair and then rolled over the desk chair for himself. He lowered himself gingerly, wincing as his knee protested. Not completely there. "Breakfast sandwich. Last night you were already anticipating a fast getaway?"

"It's actually my regular breakfast, one I can take with me. I can't count the times I've had to rush out to conduct an interview or roust the DP and grip."

"Not much different from most of my mornings. Cereal's not portable. I always have toast with my eggs, so I can stack it up if necessary. Bacon too."

"Do-it-yourself sandwich." She grinned, and this time her eyes lit with humor.

They ate and drank, speaking only of the meal. What the day would bring was a topic to avoid. Matt would bring it up soon if she didn't. For now, it was enough to chew on the idea that they had something in common. They did a lot of traveling, and they often had to eat on the go. When they got out of this jam, if she didn't hate him again—for good reason—maybe there was a chance…

Before he got too carried away with the improbable, he ditched those thoughts. After finishing his food, he took his coffee to the window. The mug was halfway to his mouth when he saw them. Across the street, five guys stood beneath the street light, their gazes concealed behind sunglasses. A dead giveaway, sunglasses in the rain. Their heads swiveled to assess the general area and the hotel entrance. Warm-up jackets, sweatshirts, bulges in the pockets. Predatory military bearing.

Hunting Nadia and him.

A heavy-set man with a buzz cut seemed to be the leader. He pointed toward 34th Street, and two guys peeled off in that direction.

Matt breathed again.

"They've found us!" Nadia stood beside him, her hand on her mouth. She gripped his arm. "This is all my fault. I knew I shouldn't, but I had to call my dad. They must've traced the call." Fear and grief warred in her gaze.

He wrapped an arm around her quaking shoulders. "Honey, I've been too tough on you about your dad. You needed to know. Tell me about it later, okay? Take a deep breath. We'll be okay. Tracking just pings on the cell tower, and there are more than three other hotels near this one. They've sent two guys to the inn on 34th, so they're still searching."

She was close to tears now. He pulled her in and wrapped his arms around her, inhaled her fresh, sweet scent. But only for a minute. They didn't have much time.

She blinked, firmed her chin and stepped back as if ready to do battle. He'd want her on his team anytime.

"DARK? FBI?"

"Not DARK officers. I'd recognize them." It was her phone that was tracked, not his. Not yet. "Not FBI either. Look at their clothing. Pressed jeans. Military shoes. Maybe some of Cardona's rebels."

"They can't search hotel rooms or wander the restaurants," she said. "So how?"

"Our pictures are probably all over the news by now. But mine has the eye patch and scars. Neither the desk clerk nor the waiter has seen you."

"Could that guy be Cardona?" She pointed toward the stocky leader.

"I've seen his picture. It's not him." The two who'd left jogged up, shaking their heads. But now he counted only four men in total. While he'd been holding Nadia, number five had vanished. "One man is missing. Maybe he's gone toward the Ritz-Carleton, but I'm not counting on it. Let's get out of here now. Sun's been up for a half hour, but in this gloom, we ought to be nearly invisible in our raingear."

Nadia stuffed down her dread and stowed it and her meager belongings in the backpack with Matt's stuff. Because of the weather, he wore jeans and the sweatshirt. She again had put on jeans, the seedstitch pullover and new gray cross trainers to take the place of her more recognizable red ones. She'd pulled her hair back into a loose bun at her nape to keep it out of the way. Their hooded rain jackets would protect them from the rain and searching eyes.

In five minutes they were out the door.

"The back stairs." The pack slung on his shoulder, Matt headed left down the hall.

She followed close behind, stretching her legs to

keep up. He wasn't letting his gimpy knee slow him. He must be worried the fifth guy was inside the hotel.

As the stairwell door whooshed shut behind them, she shuddered at the mental image of Matt's fall down the last flight of stairs. If she said anything about the possibility he'd slip and tumble again, he'd take it wrong. Well, no, he wouldn't, but she'd rather not damage whatever was developing between them or insult his abilities. Matt was anything but incapable. He was always prepared and possessed a situational awareness and vigilance she'd only read about in thrillers. He considered ahead every eventuality.

"Wait," she said.

He swung toward her, his gaze wary, scanning the small space with cool efficiency. His hand went to the pistol in his jacket pocket. "Did you hear something?"

"No, no, it's not that." She hooked the pack from his shoulder. "You need to be ready in case, well, who knows. The backpack might be in the way." She sent him a level stare, crossing mental fingers he accepted her reasoning.

"Good call." He headed down, holding the railing and watching his step.

Even though they wore soft-soled shoes, their footfalls echoed in the hard-walled stairwell. The pack was heavy, but she made it the seven flights down without dropping it or having to stop and rest.

One hand on the door handle, he said, "To the left is the exit to the terrace restaurant. Too rainy and too early for anybody to be out there. We'll stay on the river side. When we make it to 36th Street, we ought to be in the clear. Pack's not too heavy?"

She shook her head, too winded to speak.

"I'll take it as soon as we see who or what's outside." He grinned and kissed her lightly. "Thanks for taking care of me."

She sputtered a breathy laugh. Her ruse hadn't fooled him one bit.

She noted only service personnel in this back hallway of the lobby, and none of them looked their way. Matt peered through the smoky glass door to the terrace. "Looks clear. We need to move fast but not look furtive."

Her heart clattered, but she hauled in deep breaths, readying herself. "Got it."

He pushed through the stairwell door, and they hurried to the terrace exit. Outside, a gust of wind blew the mist and cold drizzle into her face. She wiped her eyes. Matt halted their progress with a raised hand, and his head turned as he checked the flagstone terrace.

An easy place to be jumped, she observed, open to the river for the view, but privacy hedges blocked both sides.

"Okay," Matt murmured. "Stay close."

She didn't need to be told twice. Did she ever want to glue herself to his side.

As they reached the terrace edge, a man stepped out from the hedge.

Adrenaline roared in Nadia's ears. She halted and gripped Matt's forearm. The fifth man, it had to be. Nearly Matt's height, but not as broad shouldered. He wore a knit cap with a short bill. He pushed it farther back on his head, revealing his features.

She gasped. *I know him*.

He pulled a pistol from his left jacket pocket. His face held a blank expression. "Stop there."

Matt pushed Nadia away to his right and moved left,

separating them. He planted his feet apart and flexed his fingers. His eyes never left the man, who was barely five feet away. "Who are you? What do you want?"

"You will come with me." The man raised the gun higher, but his gaze jumped from one to the other, as if he were now doubtful of his control, uncertain where to aim.

"Nadia, get down. Now!"

Matt's command turned the man toward him.

Nadia swung the backpack. The heavy weight slammed against the man's arm full force. He staggered and dropped the gun.

Matt pounced, landing a powerful blow to the man's jaw. Another punch took them both to the ground.

She scooped up the pistol and dashed out of the way.

The men grappled in the grass until Matt powered a chop to the guy's throat. He fell back, making choking noises. Another blow to the temple and he lay still.

"Is he…?"

Matt shook his head. He went through the man's pockets, took out his phone and removed the battery. Pocketing it, he left the phone and pushed to his feet. "He's breathing. Just unconscious. Help me drag him out of sight."

Nadia reached for his feet and lifted. "Are you all right?"

"Never better. Since yesterday, I've wanted to slug somebody. Finally got my chance." He hoisted up the guy by his shoulders and grinned. "You nailed him damn hard yourself, honey. Saved us both."

"I had to do something."

"But next time I tell you to get down, do it. This could've ended much worse."

"Yes, yes, I understand. I will. But the attacker… I, he—"

"Not here. Let's beat it before he wakes up."

They stashed the man beneath a shrub and hurried toward the Potomac. Matt chucked the pistol far out into the water before they booked it toward the lights of the Key Bridge.

Chapter Sixteen

MATT DRANK HIS coffee and watched Nadia enjoy her macchiato, something sweet that should revive her while he used one of his burner phones to search online for news. Although she hadn't complained, she was flagging after their hour trek. Her eyes were nearly closed, but her occasional sexy hums were reviving a vital part of him. He shifted in his seat.

After taking off along the shoreline away from the hotel, they'd kept up a good pace on 36th and then 35th. Zigs and zags through a townhouse neighborhood then took them to Wisconsin Avenue north, away from where the men had been searching. On their long walk, she shared her conversation with her dad. More than he overheard.

"As she was dying, Mom had made him promise to tell me about her being pregnant before they met, but he kept putting it off," she said, sniffing back tears.

"Why now?" Although he feared he knew the answer.

"More than one reason. He didn't say so, but he's afraid of another attack." She shook her head as if to dispel violent images against her frail father. "But there's more. Maybe worse. Tests at the hospital found advanced prostate cancer."

Matt pulled her under a shop awning and held her while she cried. Her father was seriously ill and could die in prison—and not too long in the future. "When we get out of this, I'll see what I can do to get him moved," he told her as they moved on.

His knee ached by the time they found this coffee shop by its smell of fresh donuts, bread and pastries. The place was full, but they had lucked into a back table covered with an honest-to-God red-checked cloth as a couple had been leaving.

Nadia wiped crumbs from her lips now and fluttered her napkin. "Great cranberry muffin. Good mix of sweet and tart."

Like you. He liked that she appreciated food and didn't pick at it like some women, but he knew better than to blurt that out.

She nodded toward the phone. "What are you finding on that thing?"

"Not much about the bombing, but some good news." He held the screen so she could see it. News footage showed the princess being wheeled out of the hospital and helped into a limo.

Hope glistened in her eyes. "Oh, oh, she's on the mend. I'm so relieved." Her expression sank. She lowered her voice. "But doesn't that put her in danger again?"

He swallowed his bite of donut. "She'll have protection, but yes, and it means we need answers. And fast."

Along with the info about her father during their trek here, she'd told him she knew their attacker. "You're positive about that guy working at the embassy?"

"Security guard, yes. I recognized the blond hair and his eyes. Mean and squinty. I don't recall his name though. He and a couple of the others carried boxes for me when I moved into my basement space. I wondered at the time why it wasn't maintenance workers, but now I think Renzo wanted his guards to keep an eye on me. Afraid I'd steal the silverware or something." Her green eyes widened. "Could those men searching for us be Modena Security?"

"Possible but a stretch. Foreign embassy personnel have no legal standing to investigate or make arrests on U.S. soil. Captain Renzo likely has input, but it's the Feds in the field."

"And you don't think those guys are FBI."

"Not Secret Service either, even with the military footwear." A possibility hit him. "Rebels. Squinty could be with the rebels. Could be the traitor." *Fuck.* He hit the table with his fist, rocking their crockery and drawing unwanted attention.

She steadied both mugs and smiled an apology at their startled neighbors. To him she said, "Don't beat yourself up about that. You didn't have much time."

"Thanks. It helps, but..." He jabbed stiff fingers through his hair.

"And it makes more sense the traitor is or was someone higher up in the embassy." Her mouth tightened as she thought. "Before everything went to hell, did you suspect anyone?"

"Nothing definite. I had my contact officer dig deeper about a few. DARK regs say I can't tell you, but given our circumstances, why not." She had good instincts about people. Not counting about him. "George Ingel, for one."

"Ah." She pursed her lips, plumping them. He wanted to kiss her. "He's been outspoken about ending the monarchy. Does all that jolly humor hide betrayal?"

"I've wondered the same. If he's involved with the rebels, patriotism is an unlikely motive. More likely ambition."

"He was talking with Sari in the office as we were getting ready for the interview. Unless something was in his suit jacket pocket, he brought in nothing and left with nothing. With so many people around, I can't see how he could've planted an explosive. He's been in and out of her office many times, so I suppose that means nothing." She picked at the crumbs on her empty plate and swung her crossed leg back and forth.

"He hurried out with Alina Greco and Dominic Traynor. The explosive DARK thinks was C-4, a plastic compound. It could've been in there for days waiting to be triggered with a specific cell phone signal."

"Like people think we did." Her expression was purposeful but strained. Her attempt at calm and thoughtful was costing her. "More likely that Kelmen or Brody brought it in that day in some filming equipment."

He covered her hand with his. "Sorry."

She nodded and squeezed his fingers. "I agree, although I hate it. If not Ingel, who else?"

"Dominic Traynor, the prime minister's man sent to aid Sarika in trade talks. Or to spy on her for him. Also a man with ambition. But who in public life doesn't have ambition?"

"I got the feeling something romantic was going on between him and Sarika. But she's never said anything." Her expression brightened. "At least we know she's on the mend."

"The only good thing in this… mess." He'd started to say *clusterfuck*, which was a better description. But there was another good thing. Nadia. And the something going on between them, albeit temporary. He wouldn't let himself dwell on the reasons for that.

Other than the embassy guard, they had nada. If only he could fucking get at what DARK had dug up on Ingel and Traynor or anybody. If only he could find out where Cardona was hiding. He must have something else planned, but what? Dammit, the inability to talk to Stratton sliced through Matt. He blew out a harsh breath. Looking up from his clenched fists, he saw Nadia studying him with that focused intensity he knew well. She'd come up with another idea. "What?"

"Maybe Squinty's not the only traitor. He could be only a minion. And suppose there are two, even three people tight with the rebels."

"DARK's source was definite on only one. It doesn't seem likely Cardona could turn more than one person and embed them in the embassy at the same time."

"Could Squinty have made the phone call that set us up?"

"The call came from outside the embassy," he said. "Doesn't mean he's not a traitor. And we don't know who *answered* that call. Could've been him." Shit, more he didn't know.

"So say he's with the rebels. Why would Cardona want his men to shoot us?"

Matt shook his head. "Remember what Squinty said—'You will come with me.' Those guys want to grab us up, not kill us." *Yet.* But he wouldn't say that. "Besides, his weapon's safety was on."

"Same question. Why?" She set down her mug and held up her hand. "Okay, Cardona and his cronies framed us for the bombing. They probably expected the blast to kill us along with… everyone else, which would leave no one for authorities to question. Could Cardona fear we know something?"

"Makes sense. Good thinking. You could be a DARK investigator."

Her smile lighted her eyes and put color in her cheeks. "Why thank you, Officer Leoni, but I'll stick with my documentary." She faltered. "If I still have a gig."

"We'll get through this. With a little more info, I can come up with a plan."

She stopped the leg gymnastics. Peered under the table, behind her, under his chair, and grinned. "And where will you find this info?"

"In Maryland. Buddy of mine, Tiana Andre, is a DARK tech officer. Woman's a genius at anything computer. Maybe I can talk her into digging into DARK's probe, and I'll set her on Cardona's trail." Tiana was as big on following regs as Stratton, but she'd understand their plight and not turn them in. He hoped. And he hoped her current squeeze, Ritter, wasn't there.

Her brow creased, and she tilted her head. "You sure she won't turn us in?"

"Nah, she'll help us, but we have to wait until she gets home from work. Maybe around seven, maybe later." He'd save the rest for later, for when Tiana couldn't back out.

Nadia's skeptical expression hadn't eased, but she nodded. Then she raised both hands, gesturing at the thinning crowd in the coffee shop. "We can't sit here all day eating muffins and donuts."

He pushed back his chair and stood. "Hey, what does anyone do on a rainy day? We go to the movies. We can make out in the back row."

****

Nadia shivered in the night air. Thank goodness the skies had cleared. They stood in the dark, watching Tiana Andre's deck and apartment windows. Matt wanted to be sure no one was inside but her before ringing the bell. He said he'd been there with a few colleagues for a cookout, so he knew the layout. The man must keep a map in his head of everywhere he'd ever been. The lights were on, but that was all they'd discerned.

They'd spent a few hours at a Star Wars marathon, a great escape. A few other people lounged scattered around the theater, but they had the back row to themselves. They disagreed about nearly everything—the best movie, the best character, the best special effects. But they both hated the episode with Jar Jar Binks.

She caught him covering his right eye, checking how much he could see with the damaged left. Her silent prayer winged upward. She didn't ask, but laid her hand on his arm.

"About the same. For now," he whispered. "It's coming back."

She smiled now at the memory of *making out* in the back row. They'd argued about that too.

"Making out?" she accused. "Is this the sixties? Next you'll call it necking."

In the theater's darkness, his eyes were midnight, his features hard planes and angles. He curved his arm, strong and warm around her shoulders. His chuckle vibrated against her temple. "So let's get it on. Then we can call it a real date instead of hiding out."

Before his last words could yank her back to reality,

he pressed his mouth to hers and delved inside with his tongue, salty with the popcorn they were sharing. Her blood was pumping, and she heard herself whimper before she dredged up the strength to end the kiss. Breathing hard, he tipped his head against hers and returned his gaze to the current movie. She couldn't have come up with the title if it had been the clue to the traitor.

The rain had slowed to a few drops by the time they emerged. The subway took them to Dupont Circle's art galleries, and later a ride-hailing service dropped them at an Italian restaurant in downtown Silver Spring.

"Looks like we're in the clear." He forked up a hunk of his lasagna. "Fewer surveillance possibilities in the 'burbs. The only hitch I foresee could be at Tiana's."

Her left eyebrow leaped upward. Goosebumps prickled on her forearms. Had she become too complacent, mentally blocking the dangers? She set down her full fork of shrimp marinara. "Hitch?"

"Crap." His broad shoulders rounded and twin red spots appeared on his cheekbones. "I should've told you earlier, but I figured you'd balk. Tiana's all I got."

He'd kept something from her, but how bad could it be? "Spit it out."

He took a long drink of red wine. Fortifying himself? "Tiana's dating, hell, practically engaged to Ken Ritter."

Nadia's ears rang with Matt's last words and her pulse scrambled. "So why would she—"

"Help us? Because she and I are old friends, even before he came on the scene, and because she knows Ritter's doggedness, even ruthlessness on a case."

They'd discussed the alternatives for a few minutes. Argued actually, until agreeing there were no alternatives. The longer they stayed in the wind, he said, the worse it looked. So she'd agreed.

After the meal, they'd walked here to this garden apartment complex.

"You should've told me earlier, you know," she said now.

"No shit. I'm a coward. I tried a couple of times, but couldn't get out the words. Until I had to say it. I'm sorry."

He held out his arms, and she walked into them. She knew his scent, the rhythm of his breathing, the gentle way he touched her, held her. He was smart and funny and loyal and sexy as hell. He understood her as no one else had. She saw the mirror of her loneliness in his dark eyes. She knew now that he hadn't used her five years ago, that he'd genuinely been attracted to her. And she no longer felt she was betraying her dad.

No other man had ever said to her he was sorry, not even Dad. It was enough to tip her over the edge and acknowledge the truth. Even though there was no future in it, she'd fallen for him.

"Okay, honey," he said, taking her by the hand, "here we go. We wait any longer, she'll turn off the lights and go to bed."

Chapter Seventeen

THE DOOR OPENED before Matt could ring the bell. Finger to her lips, Tiana beckoned them inside. Using a remote, she clicked the door locks. They stood in a small foyer that opened into a combo living and kitchen area.

Hands on her slim hips, she wagged her head, setting her topknot of little black braids dancing. She favored jeans and brightly colored tailored shirts. Today's was red. "What took you so long? You've been standing out there in the cold for forty-five minutes. You must be frozen!" Her gaze fell on Nadia, and her brow knit in apparent confusion.

He couldn't help laughing. "What was I thinking, Q? I should know you'd have surveillance." Hell, Tiana probably even knew why they were here.

She threw up her hands. "Simon calls Janna that. Don't *you* start with me!"

She was staring at Nadia again. Crap, he'd been yakking and hadn't made introductions. "Tiana Andre, meet Nadia Parker. I guess you already know we've gone AWOL."

Nadia's hand was trembling but she shook when the other woman offered. He put his arm around her shoulders and pulled her closer. She probably feared Ritter was lurking in a closet.

"I do know, sort of, at least what has leaked into my

lab over coffee and what I saw on the news. Ditching the eye patch and covering the scars must've helped you hide out. Come on in and get comfortable. Then we'll talk."

Tiana took their jackets and ushered them into a large living room separated from the kitchen by an eating bar. Simple furniture in neutral colors sat on a dark green carpet. On the walls over full bookshelves, paintings of Caribbean mountain villages hung beside geometric prints. Maybe Tiana's warm welcome and the pleasant space would calm Nadia's fears.

She got them settled on the sofa and turned up the gas fireplace. After bringing drinks—pinot noir for Nadia and her and a bottle of microbrew for him—she sat across from them on a matching chair.

"Sorry I was staring," she said, smiling at Nadia, "but you look so much like that poor injured Princess Sarika, for a minute I thought you were her. I saw online that she's been released from the hospital."

"I guess there's some resemblance," Matt said. Maybe it was the hair, pulled back like Sarika's. Or maybe it was that they were both blonde, about the same height and build. Not enough so he'd ever confuse the two women. Nadia was outgoing and animated while Sarika was cool and reserved.

"We saw that news too. I'm relieved she's improved that much." Nadia took a sip of her wine and set the goblet on the side table. She wound her fingers together in her lap. One foot tapped on the carpet. "We're friends. The resemblance is less obvious when we're side by side." Her hand flew to her throat as she blinked hard, clearly still fretting about Princess Sarika's safety.

Tiana exchanged a glance with Matt, and he nodded

his encouragement. She set down her wine goblet. "So what can I do for you two?"

Matt had one backup plan if Tiana said no. Simon Byrne, DARK's resident rebel, might help them, but that would mean another delay, another night on the run, more stress for Nadia. And more time for Cardona to plot another attempt on the princess's life.

He explained their situation, why he'd cut himself off from DARK and was protecting Nadia. Especially why she feared the agency. "Before I go further, I need your promise you won't turn us in and won't tell Ken any of this." He held his breath while she stared at him, the wheels turning behind her sharp gray eyes.

"I know how he is on a case, especially on your father's, Nadia," Tiana said finally. "I won't say anything to him. As far as I'm concerned, neither of you was ever here. So?"

Nadia's hands relaxed, and he pressed his knee against hers. He laid out his explanation, and then said, "Whether or not you can find what I need, we'll have to go in soon. Staying on the run with no resources is getting us nowhere."

Tiana led them down a short hall to an office, where computers, monitors and other humming equipment occupied a long desktop on the back wall. A few passwords and clicked keys took her into DARK's case file on the Modena rebel group. "I hope Simon's gone home by now because I'm using his login. Here's what they have on Dominic Traynor and George Ingel." She pulled over another desk chair for Matt and turned the monitor his way.

He scrolled through the files while Nadia stood to one side chewing her lower lip. "Ingel is angling to run for parliament against the current prime minister. Speculation is he wants to be the next prime. That makes Traynor no friend of his. Nothing in Traynor's file indicates disloyalty to the royal family or the government. Dammit, this gives us zip." He turned the monitor back to Tiana. She was lucky he didn't toss it out the window. He got up to pace the room.

"Who's the other person?"

He drew a calming breath. Her matter-of-fact tone eased his temper. "The leader of the Modena rebels, Sandor Cardona. Reports said he came into the States from Canada and is now in the District. I'd like you to find proof."

"Let's see if I can find him nearby."

Nadia stopped his pacing with a hand on his shoulder. "Didn't you say DARK had video surveillance of the embassy? Would Cardona be bold enough to go there, maybe to scope it out?"

"Bold enough, arrogant enough. Yeah, it's possible." He cupped her chin, brushed a kiss on her lips, and she smiled against them. He'd needed that connection with her, her scent, the feel of her. The revelation was a jolt from a live wire, that this one woman caused such need in him. Or was it the intense emotion of their situation? Beat the hell out of him.

"Worth a try." He held Nadia against his side and was gratified when she eased even closer. "A team set up surveillance cameras on the day I started my gig. That was Monday. Four damn days ago. It's a busy street."

"Let's see." Tiana clicked away for a few minutes. The monitor showed stills of people on the street in front of and near the building.

Matt plopped into the chair again and scrolled

through the images. Behind him Nadia's shoes were scuffing on the carpet. Now she was the one pacing. The images were clear, but it was hard to see faces. Men, women, delivery people, bicyclists, an occasional skateboarder. He skipped the men whose heads were bent over their phones. "The images are clear, but there are so many people."

"If I have a description, I can narrow the possibilities." Tiana looked up, a questioning expression on her face.

"Average height. Lean build. Narrow face. His passport photo shows him with a thin mustache and a lot of dark hair. But he could be disguised." Fuck.

"Passport? Hold on." Shortly, a second monitor displayed Cardona's passport photo. "That him?"

Nadia bent to the image, peered at it a long moment. She sucked in a breath. "I've seen this man."

Matt shot to his feet and grabbed her hand. "Cardona? Where?"

"Remember when we were in the mall pub, I had a déjà vu about a couple at the bar?"

Yeah, he sort of did. His pulse kicked up. "Sure."

"It was a vague memory, an impression of another couple at a bar near the embassy. Not the one we ran to, but in the opposite direction. Last week, Friday, I think. Yes, the day after I set up shop at the embassy. At the time I thought it was a date or something benign, but now…"

"Now what? Who did you see?"

"I was there with Sari's admin Pascale. I saw this man there, Cardona. He had the bushy brown hair but no mustache. I'm sure it was him. That narrow face and long nose. I thought at the time how much he looked like a wolf. That's why I remembered him."

Tiana played with the image and shortly Cardona reappeared without the facial hair. "Like this?"

Matt angled his head to see the new Cardona better. A wolf, maybe. More like a jackal.

"That's him. Definitely," Nadia said. "He was leaning back against the bar, facing me. My fingers itched for a camera because the two of them were perfectly framed. That bar is only a couple blocks from the embassy." Her eyes rounded. "He could've been plotting the bombing then."

So the rebel leader was in town and close. She thought it was a date, so not Ingel or Traynor. "Did you know the other person? A woman?"

"That's why I noticed him. He was having drinks with George Ingel's admin."

Matt dropped onto his chair, hard. "Alina Greco?" His mind raced. DARK's intel indicated the mole was one of the diplomats or an emissary. He never suspected a secretary. Especially not the Barbie wannabe. Cardona's lover? Co-conspirator? What was her motive? For now that didn't matter.

"Alina could've been the one to set off the bomb." Nadia's eyes were bleak. "If I'd known... if I'd suspected...." She shook her head and her mouth twisted into a grimace.

He tucked away the puzzle. He'd work on it later. He stood and embraced her, drew a finger down her cheek. "She was on her phone when she left the inner office. I think it's a safe bet she triggered the bomb. Nadia, you're not clairvoyant. You recognized Cardona now and linked him to Alina."

"So this is helpful?" Tiana's gaze bounced between

them.

He erupted in a bitter laugh. "Helpful? No shit. This is monumental. This is what I was at the embassy to find—the traitor, the mole working with the rebels. Thank you isn't enough, but you have to know that you were a key step in finding her."

"You're welcome, but is it enough? Is there more you need?" she said.

Finally he could take action. But going in meant risk to Nadia, something he swore to avoid. He pushed to his feet, suddenly energized with an idea. "I doubt you can help. I have to call my contact with this info, but it means we'll be picked up and separated for debriefing. Nadia may be accused." He couldn't say to Ritter's girlfriend that it meant she'd face that bastard again. He pulled Nadia to him.

She trembled in the curve of his arm. Unshed tears glittered in her eyes, but her chin came up. "I can take it. This is crucial. These rebels murdered three people. They have to be stopped before they try again to kill Sari."

Tiana looked thoughtful. She glanced at a gadget on the desk. "What if your call to DARK couldn't be traced to your location?"

"I take it you have some electronic voodoo to offer, but I don't want to compromise your follow-the-rules rep."

"Consider it part of my beta testing. The technology's something I've been working on for a while, a ping bouncer. Not a sexy tech name, but I'm working on that. If I enter your phone number into it, your call will appear to come from three or more cell towers away."

His nerves jangled with the possibilities. He could

call in safely. Identifying Alina as the traitor would prove Nadia was innocent. He had more proof, but the thought of using it twisted a dagger inside his chest. It would mean the end of his relationship with her. He cleared his throat. "Does the agency know about this device?"

"My boss will when I'm finished tinkering." Tiana grinned. "I expect a big bonus."

"Not a problem. Are you sure it'll work?"

Her calm expression gave no indication of misgivings about her invention. "If it doesn't, we'll both be compromised. Are you game?"

Chapter Eighteen

NADIA CLIMBED ONTO one of the two stools at Tiana's eating bar. Aromas of roast chicken and lemons wafted from a casserole dish on the counter. She accepted a little more pinot in her glass. "It's a nice wine." The women had left Matt in the office to make his call in private. Nadia glanced in that direction.

"Matt's a good guy." Tiana added to her goblet and sat on the adjacent stool. "You can trust him. I see how he is with you, and how you look at him. Great that even under these circumstances you've found each other."

Inside her, a soft, hopeful feeling warred with a fear of going all in. Irrational, but there it was. "We have a history. It's complicated."

"What relationship isn't?" Tiana looked as if she were about to share something about her and Ken Ritter, but instead she lifted her goblet and drank. "How is it that you and the Modena princess are old friends?"

Nadia told her the same thing she'd told Matt, that her mother and Sari's mother, the queen, were friends, and that the two girls had roomed together in college.

They chatted about college life and Nadia majoring in film. Then Tiana asked, "Did you and the princess ever pretend to be each other?"

Nadia brightened at the happy memory. "Sometimes we wore each other's clothes and spoofed people, yes."

"People. Like guys on dates?"

"Sure. Once or twice. I can do her boarding-school British accent, but she can't do American, so it was tricky." She grinned, remembering the time a guy caught out Sari because of her terrible American accent. "Our hair was almost the same color back then. These days, Sari has hers lightened a few shades."

"More princess-like, I suppose," Tiana said.

Nadia agreed and set her glass away, refusing the other woman's offer of more. Tapping fingers on the bar's granite top, she swiveled toward the hallway. "This call is taking a long time. What if—"

"No what ifs," Tiana said. "They're probably going over all the possibilities."

"Or else Matt's contact has started a search for him. For us."

"Don't sweat it. My ping bouncer works, and Matt's the best. People talk at work, no matter how super secret the agency's supposed to be. He's proven himself an excellent DARK officer, and he's worked so hard to recover after his terrible injury so he can get back to field officer status. He's risking a lot by running with you, you know."

Emotion clogged Nadia's throat. "Everything. He's risking *everything*."

She hated this helpless feeling. Yes, she'd moved closer to their goal by recognizing Cardona, but she was used to making plans and doing the organizing. The conversation turned to the afternoon's Star Wars marathon, but her mind kept working. If only there was something more she could do….

****

When Matt returned from his call, he stopped in the hallway, enjoying hearing the women talk like old friends. Aside from the breakthrough, bringing Nadia here was a big plus.

Unless DARK or Cardona's thugs arrived with guns drawn at Tiana's apartment, they were safe. He'd called Byrne, figuring he'd go along more readily than straight-arrow Stratton. Even Byrne had been pissed as hell at first, but calmed down as Matt explained. They also kicked around scenarios for how the bombing had gone down, but came to no conclusions.

Finally, Matt had asked Byrne to persuade Ritter not to accuse Nadia. The other man had agreed, saying both he and Stratton would work on Ritter.

Matt joined the women. "Looks like we're good to go. I'll phone in the morning and arrange for Nadia and me to be collected." He checked the clock on the kitchen wall. "Alina Greco will be under surveillance in a matter of minutes. Picking her up tonight might've alerted Cardona. With any luck, she'll lead officers to him and we won't need a trap."

He stood beside Nadia and wrapped an arm around her shoulders. "I explained about you identifying Cardona meeting with her. That key bit of information should be enough for Ritter to back off interrogating you."

Clasping the hand on her shoulder, she turned and met his gaze. "If it's not, I'll deal." Her voice was strong, but anxiety was stark in her eyes.

Techno music erupted from Tiana's jeans pocket. She pulled out her phone. "I have to take this. That's my dad. Help yourself to a beer." She disappeared down the hall and into a bedroom. The door shut with a soft click.

He brought his bottle back and took the stool she'd vacated.

"That it? Or just all you can reveal?" Nadia said.

He shrugged. "DARK has intel that the next attempt on the princess will be at a charity ribbon cutting Tuesday afternoon."

"The Capital Refugee Resettlement Center," she said. "She's been a big donor on behalf of Modena, where a lot of refugees wash up on the beaches. But she must still be weak. How can she…?" She looked away, lost in thought, or in sorrow for her friend.

"Probably she won't be strong enough to attend. Stratton said as much, that they couldn't allow her to set herself up as a target anyway."

"I can do it," Nadia said.

His hand jerked, and beer splashed on his shirt. He hardly noticed the icy wetness. "Excuse me?"

"I can be the target. DARK can set it up. I look enough like Sari, can even change my hair and wear her clothes. I can take her place and help trap the rebel leader."

Shit in a shoebox. "Honey, no. You've helped already by recognizing him. You can't do this." He set away the beer bottle and grasped her hands. Not trembling. Like her determined gaze, they were steady.

"You don't get it, Matt. *I* was the one who brought the phony crew into the embassy. Those men and Pascale died, and Sari nearly did."

"Because *those men* brought the bomb in, not you. And here's another flash. You probably saved Sarika's life by moving her chair over by the glass doors and keeping the curtain open. The blast threw her onto the balcony, and the overturned chair shielded her from the worst of the flaming debris."

She shook her head and tugged on her hands, but he

held onto her. "I want, no, I *need* to do something to help, something to take away the weight of responsibility for that damn bomb. I can be the—"

"Goat? And put yourself in the crosshairs, defenseless? Not gonna happen. DARK would never agree to such a fucking stu— ah, risky idea."

The look she leveled at him could've frozen Lake Michigan. "We'll see."

****

Nadia tossed her rain jacket on the back of a chair and toed off her sneakers. Matt's mood had turned blacker than a fade-out since they left Tiana's. Difficulty finding a hotel room this late on a Friday night hadn't improved matters. With both of them on phones—new burners—finally they booked a vacancy at this small brick inn near Dupont Circle.

DARK would pick them up in the morning, and agents would probably separate them, her for questioning and Matt for what they call debriefing, mere semantics for what was the same as questioning. He'd assured her that his colleagues would prevent her interrogation from being conducted by somebody other than Ken Ritter. Maybe. She'd be ready… as long as she could have this one night, this last night with Matt. But not one of anger and argument. She didn't dare think the L word, but if they could make love with tenderness and trust, their—what, affair, interlude?—would give her, *them*, fond memories. The idea of never being with him again scraped her heart. *Buck up, Nadie*, as Dad would say.

She turned toward Matt, who'd shot the locks but still stood in the foyer. "David Martinez, Paul Malik, and now Josh Bruno. Just how many of those fake IDs do you have?" And credit cards, she could've added. But she was trying for light and playful.

"Enough." He bit the words between clenched teeth. The veins were nearly popping out of his neck. He stalked—no other way to describe that stiff and, yes, pissed-off stride—to the pair of windows and pulled the drapes.

Her attempt at light? Major fail. She wanted his smile back, the smile that made her heart race. She was right about taking Sari's place, she knew it. She could help her mother's country, protect her dearest friend from further dangers and clear suspicion from herself. If Matt couldn't understand that— No, that was wrong. He did understand because he knew her, and his intensity now meant he was afraid for her. At the thought, deep longing welled up within her.

She rummaged in the backpack for her things while he performed security checks—bathroom, closet, desk, lamps—with the bug detector that masqueraded as a pen, invented by another DARK tech wizard named Janna, she'd learned. Maybe routine would soothe the beast within. If not that, then maybe the room's earth tones, the fireplace, the oriental carpet, the soft glow of the desk lamp.

He ripped off his rain jacket, tossed it on the room's upholstered chair. The sweatshirt followed. He kicked away his sneakers as if they were live alligators eating his toes. One bounced away into a corner.

Not soothed. Not one bit.

She had to get him talking. She approached him and placed a hand on his arm. His fists were clenched, the forearm muscles bulging. Quite tantalizingly. But instead of continuing to stare, she placed her hands on them. She clucked her tongue. "Such taut muscles. Are you about to go all superhero on me?"

He chuffed and met her gaze with a scowl, but his bunched muscles relaxed beneath her fingers. "Dammit, Nadia, what you intend is fucking dangerous." He bent and pressed his forehead to hers. "I don't want to lose... I mean, we have something together I don't want to lose when it's over. I don't want *us* to be over. I care about you, for you... a lot. I don't want you hurt. Or..." He heaved a sigh, ran his hands up and down her upper arms.

His words, wrenched from deep within him, tightened her throat. The gentleness in his touch and in his chocolate gaze started pulsing between her legs. She'd never wanted a man the way she wanted Matt, but she wasn't ready to reveal more than he had. "I care for you too. I've let the past go. I don't know where this— us being together—is going, but I want to find out."

"But dammit, Nadia—"

She stopped him with a finger on his lips. "You're afraid for me, and I love that, but I have to do this if DARK will go for it." When he said nothing, his impressive erection tight against her belly, she knew what he wanted at the moment. "Why didn't you accept Tiana's offer to stay there? Because you wanted to keep yelling at me?"

"No," he growled. But the corners of his mouth turned upward.

"Then why?" She slid her arms around his waist and tugged his T-shirt from his jeans. "Was it because of this?" She ran her palms up his bare back, being careful with the healing scabs. She danced her fingers along his spine, reveling in his solid power. Just touching him like this made her insides melt.

He sucked in a harsh breath and grabbed her arms, pulled her hands away from their seductive play. His dark eyes flashed with barely banked fire. "You're not going to change my mind. Setting yourself up as bait is a nutty idea. Too risky."

"I know." His mouth came down on hers like lightning. *Yes!*

She gave up control to him as one hand on the back of her head held her in place while the other gripped her butt, clamping her against him. The sleek glide of his tongue against her lips coaxed them open, sending a spill of desire throughout her as she tangled her tongue with his, tasting of cinnamon gum. Needing to touch every plane and angle of him, she tugged at the soft cotton fabric until he pulled it over his head and tossed it away. He was all heat and hardness and musky male scent. Both breathless, they clung to each other as his jeans and boxers were shucked and then her outer clothes and panties. He flicked open her bra and threw it aside, palmed her breasts and laved them with his tongue until they gleamed and beaded from his caresses and the cool air. Her breath came hurried and shallow, and she could barely stand.

She threw back the king bed's covers, and he drew her down onto the smooth sheets and on top of him. They kissed with such heat and hunger, her head reeled and her body thrummed with desire. She writhed against him, pressed kisses to his lightly furred chest, to his flat nipples, to the pulse beating below his throat. She'd known passion before, but nothing so all-encompassing as how only this man, more than any other she'd ever known, could saturate her senses, could make her feel a pull like the tide, could make her want more than she could have….

His heated length strained against her belly, and when she rubbed herself against him and scraped her nails along the base of his spine, he groaned and arched his back. "I like a woman who knows what she wants." His voice rasped but contained a smile. *At last.*

He turned them to face each other, and his fingers delved into the moisture between her thighs. She went perfectly still, all her circuits tangled, and ripplets of heat surged through her. "Matt!"

"I know." He slid downward and kissed her intimately with his mouth and tongue, tasting and flicking and exploring. Quivers shuddered up her thighs and the climax took her, a shattering burning that lasted only an instant, like lightning. She gasped, her breathing shallow and hurried.

"There's more," he murmured as he moved upward, sheathed himself, and slid into her.

Her inner muscles tightened around him as she drew him in deeper. "Yes, oh yes." She loved his dark liquid gaze, his heat, his salty male scent, how even his touch made her insides melt, how he took his time pleasuring her, blurring the boundaries of her body joining his. But in the recesses of her mind fear lurked. Was she getting in too deep, setting herself up for pain and heartbreak? He moved, seeking, stroking again and again until he drew from her a wrenching wave of pleasure that dissolved all thought.

Chapter Nineteen

IN THE MORNING, they made love again, slowly, taking their time and savoring every touch, every stroke, every sensation. Afterward, Matt gathered Nadia into his arms and held her, memorizing the feel of her skin against his, her hand on his chest, the thump of her heart against his side. Whatever happened today would change everything, and not for the better. Thinking about her setting herself up as a target for the rebels made his chest hurt.

After a quick breakfast in the inn's dining room, he phoned Cole Stratton, and within twenty minutes they were seated in the back of an official SUV headed for DARK headquarters. He recognized the two officers who'd collected them, but hadn't worked with either. The woman drove and the man locked them in. Both stone-faced and taciturn.

Nadia's hand strangled his, but she said nothing, only jiggled her foot and worried her lower lip. Nervous fidgeting and not her normal animation, but her chin was up and firm. He forced himself to remain expressionless and still.

All too soon, the nondescript granite-faced building loomed ahead. Ironically, or appropriately, depending on a person's viewpoint, the Domestic Antiterrorism Risk Corps was situated equidistant between Homeland Security and the International Spy Museum. Once inside the basement garage, the officers escorted them to Security, where they and Matt's pack were searched, then to an upper floor. Their escorts handed them off to Matt's teammates, Simon Byrne and Cole Stratton. Not Ken Ritter. He sent a silent thank you upward. He made quick introductions, but nobody shook hands.

"The prodigal son returns." Byrne grinned, delivering a not-so-light punch to Matt's biceps.

"Yeah, we'll see." He might lose his job—if he was lucky, not worse—but maybe Nadia would be questioned and her nutty idea dismissed. He introduced her to his colleagues.

Stratton nodded to her. "Ms. Parker, Officer Byrne will be debriefing you. Officer Leoni will come with me."

She turned to Matt, and he said, "Standard procedure. It'll be okay. No rubber hoses."

She didn't smile, but the stiffness in her posture eased.

"This way," Byrne said, gesturing to the right, where a long hallway led to interview rooms and offices.

Her skin seemed drawn tight over her cheekbones, but her green eyes were clear and determined as she gave Matt one last look before accompanying her interrogator or interviewer. Which, he couldn't say.

Every blood vessel pounding and fists clenched, he sent Byrne a warning look.

As the inveterate rule breaker walked away with Nadia, he sent back a cocky grin. Matt read the finger tap beside his left eye as "message received."

Stratton hitched his chin toward the other direction and started walking. Marching would be the better term. The man carried himself like he was still in the Marines.

Matt took his time following.

"Ritter will be running the meeting," Stratton said when Matt caught up to him. Don't expect him to go easy on you. When he heard you'd gone AWOL, his mood was black enough to block the sun."

Stratton's brittle tone meant he didn't approve of Ritter's hardline approach. A good sign Matt might not be staked to an anthill and flayed alive. "You mean he didn't shed tears thinking I'd gone tits up when the bomb blew?"

"If he was, he kept it to himself." He headed to the elevator. "We'll be in our usual office."

"Cole," Matt said, "I know what I did, and I'd do it again. I can take whatever Ritter lobs at me. My thanks to you and Simon for keeping him away from Nadia."

"Neither of us figured she deserved another go-around of Ritter-style interrogation. Took some fast talking, Simon's specialty. That, and General Nolan stepped in. Somebody happened to send him the report that Nadia Parker gave us the break we needed."

"Somebody, huh? Thanks, man." Stratton and Byrne were teammates Matt could count on to have his back. In a field op, so was Ritter, but not, like now, when something stuck in his craw.

Stratton nodded but said nothing more, not even a comment about the lack of an eye patch. Matt had dispensed with the scar-concealing makeup along with the patch. They entered the open office several of them shared. His desk was cleared of everything except the computer monitor and keyboard. Only one man occupied the office.

Ken Ritter stood at his desk. As usual, he wore a suit and tie, unlike the rest of them, who usually dressed mor casually, both men and women. The sun streaming in the side window shone on his pretty-boy profile. He didn't offer a hand. His eyes slashed like sabers up and down Matt's length. Matt could almost see smoke streaming from his ears. "Take a seat, Leoni."

"I'll stand." The control officer had a couple inches on Matt. No point in giving him more advantage.

Behind him, Stratton hitched a hip on his own desk. Good. He'd stayed in the room. A witness.

"Start talking. Everything, every fucking minuscule detail starting from when the crew entered Princess Sarika's office for the filming." Ritter pushed a button on a digital recorder.

Even better. Matt worked his tight jaw and began. He paced as he talked. With two exceptions, he covered the past two days—step by step through the filming prep, the bombing and their escape, their subterfuges, their locations, the men searching for them outside the hotel and the one who'd attacked them. He and Nadia had worked out a narrative that would shield Tiana. "Last night we were having dinner when Nadia spotted a couple standing at the bar. It triggered her memory of seeing Alina Greco and a man in a bar near the embassy. From her description, I suspected it might be Cardona. I located his picture in an old Modena news feed. She recognized him, said she remembered because he reminded her of a wolf. Then I called Byrne. You know the rest." Just in case, he'd found the news feed and saved the link on the burner phone.

Ritter folded his arms and regarded him with blatant mistrust. "You may have proof that Cardona's in town, and we've heard rumblings of a new plot on the princess. But what we've got doesn't help us set up a trap. You know more than you're telling me. You're up shit creek here, so spill or face consequences."

"You're blowing smoke, Ritter. I've laid it all out. I got nothing more. What about the surveillance on Alina Greco? What's that turned up?"

Ritter stuck out his chin but said nothing.

Stratton cleared his throat. "No reason you can't know. We got nada so far. Saturday morning so she's not at work, at home alone. Our equipment can't get a read on her phone conversations, and it takes time to get the phone records."

Ritter shot his cuffs and sat, glanced at the recorder, still running. "Enough. Go through it again, Leoni. This time, leave *nothing* out."

Matt remained standing. "You want the room numbers of the hotels, what we ate? You got it." He started over, went through the same info again, chapter and verse—adding room numbers and meals. If Ritter wanted to know if he and Nadia had slept together, he wouldn't get it from him. No fucking way was he talking about his relationship with her, period. "That's it. I can do this all day, but you probably have better things to do."

"How did the guys you said might be from Modena find your hotel?"

Matt expelled a long breath. He'd prepared for this, knowing the CO wouldn't be satisfied until he caught him on something. "You know Nadia's father shanked."

The other man lifted one shoulder. "Of course. So?"

Asshat. "She was worried about him. I knew that, and I warned her not to call the prison. When we spotted the creeps outside the hotel in the morning, she told me that while I was asleep, she'd called the prison from her phone, not one of the burners. The prison directed her to the hospital, where she reached her father. Those guys somehow were able to track her phone. She was damned upset about it."

"You hear her conversation with her dad, the fucking traitor?"

It was Matt's turn to shrug. He rolled over a chair from the next desk and sat, propping one ankle on the other knee. He draped an arm over the chair back. "Nah. I don't hear shit in my sleep."

Ritter asked him more questions, but Matt added nothing new to what he'd already described.

After two hours, Ritter shut off the recorder and stood. "Nadia Parker hired the bombers. She needs money for her father's appeal. She's as dirty as he is, in bed with the rebels, probably the New Dawn terrorists too. If Byrne got anything from the traitor's daughter, I'd hear by now. He's had enough time." He rounded his desk, headed for the door.

"Wait, Ken," Stratton said.

Matt's heart hit the panic button. This might be an empty threat, a ploy to get him to divulge more, but he couldn't take the chance.

He shot to his feet. Ritter had the door ajar before Matt reached him. "No, stop this. You're wrong about her." Jesus H. Christ, he'd hoped to avoid this. He grabbed the other man. Held on. "I have proof of her innocence. She's done nothing wrong." *Except to trust me.*

"Proof?" Ritter eyed Matt's hand on his forearm as if it had sullied his suit jacket. "This better be good. Verifiable."

Matt lifted his hand and stepped back. "It's on my secure DARK phone. Cole, it's in my pack. Battery too. Outside pocket."

The pack sat beside Stratton, who'd carried it into the office. He found the devices and brought them over. "A tech detected it was turned on early Friday morning somewhere in Georgetown. We had no luck tracing its location. I'm assuming now it was you at the Prospect Hotel."

Matt didn't respond. He inserted the battery and turned it on. "This is Nadia's conversation with her father." Matt opened the app and started the voice recording.

"Dad?"

"Aw, Nadie, honey. Thank God, I was so worried when I heard. Then I saw on TV... the bomb..." His voice broke.

Matt stared at the carpet as he listened to the anguish in Nadia's voice and the regret and weakness in her dad's. If Ritter or Stratton didn't tell her about the recording, Matt would even if it meant she never spoke to him again. And he'd deserve her hatred because he'd done exactly the thing she'd feared.

The voices went on, finishing up the important part.

"...let me get this out. The hurt and accusation in your eyes when you learned what I'd done and again when I was arrested cut me deeper than any knife these thugs could wield. I refused them three times. This time they didn't ask. They just jumped me."

"And now, now have you told the authorities why you were attacked, what they wanted?"

"I have, but I don't know what good it will do."

The door swung open, hitting Ritter in the back.

Matt pushed Stop.

In the opening stood Nadia. Fury painted her cheeks red. "You're despicable, you lying son of a bitch." She practically spat the words at him. "You used me, made me think—" She turned to Simon Byrne. "Get me away from that snake, that...." She held up both hands, curled into fists.

Face pale, she let Byrne lead her away, talking softly to her.

Black pain ballooned in Matt's chest, so total he had to force out words. "Is that fucking enough for you, Ritter?"

Chapter Twenty

MATT AND NINE others met Monday morning in a conference room to finalize the plans for tomorrow's refugee center ribbon cutting. The air-conditioning's mildew odor mingled with those of coffee and some dude's body spray that smelled more like skunk than seduction.

Cole Stratton, his back to the group, stood on one long side of the table, pointing to slides of the site projected on a big screen. "Alina Greco has put in for the day off tomorrow. Likely she intends to join Cardona at the refugee center, maybe beat it out of town with him. We're working with Modena Embassy Security to take her into custody before that can happen."

He was finally finishing his third run-through of their plans and assignments—positions in the crowd or above with sniper rifles. Everybody had memorized the photos of Cardona and the men known to have sneaked into the country with him.

Matt, who was to be one of several in the crowd, slumped in his chair to the screen's left at the table's end, his gaze unfocused. What his sins would cost him with DARK was yet to be determined. He'd worked yesterday with Stratton and Byrne on the layout, timing, and positioning. He took as a good sign that he was remaining on duty for this op.

On the other hand, he'd screwed up too much to ever

fix things with Nadia. He betrayed her trust, making love with her while spying on her, the worst possible transgression. He deserved this anvil weight inside that made his chest too tight for a deep breath.

Damn Ken Ritter to hell for taking her insanely risky idea to Director Nolan, and damn Nolan for agreeing to stake her out for Cardona's target practice. How they'd talked Sarika into agreeing, he had no idea. He couldn't blame Nadia for refusing to see him since the flame-out.

The taste of his loss was bitter on his tongue. Only when he was losing her did he realize the depth of his feelings for her. Only now did what she'd said about his needing to belong come back to him. He could lose his job with DARK. He'd risked everything, but his biggest regret was that he'd lost her. Her shimmering energy, her zeal for righting wrongs, her loyal heart. Damn.

By God, he would make certain she was protected. In the middle of the night, it had hit him. The planning had omitted a key component.

Ritter wasn't leading the op, or he'd probably want to stake out both of them as targets. Stratton was level-headed, although he'd made clear his worry about Matt going squirrely. Weekend time on the firing range had improved his accuracy, even sighting right eyed. And with both his 9mm and the .40 caliber. He wasn't sleeping much, but he had steady hands and could summon professional detachment, block out distractions—of all kinds.

Stratton finished up with his usual pep talk. "Troops, we want Cardona's men, but primarily we want Cardona. He's the damn key to ending all this. The key to stopping attacks on the Modena royals and the government. The key to preventing the New Dawn terrorists from getting a foothold on that island."

While Ritter argued with him about a point of logistics, Matt zoned out. When the discussion ended, he finally spoke. "Nadia will wear a Kevlar vest and a transceiver. All well and good. But not good enough."

Seated beside him, Simon Byrne raised his eyebrows. "You have a suggestion, maybe a suit of armor?"

Matt chose to ignore the jibe and answer the question. "As a matter of fact, I do. We embed a couple officers with the dignitaries near our substitute princess. Crowd size is anybody's guess. Too many civilians in the area—refugees of every nationality, supporters, street people, who knows how many clowns. The whole thing is beyond dicey. If our op turns into a shit storm, one or both officers can pull her to safety."

The small conference room went silent for a moment as his idea sank in.

Stratton remained expressionless, and then gave a brusque nod. "Should've thought of that myself. Too late to bring new personnel up to speed, so who'll—"

"I'll do it," Matt said.

Byrne snorted. Ritter rolled his eyes. Throats cleared around the table.

"No fucking way, Leoni." Stratton sank onto his chair and fixed him with a steely gaze. "You're too involved." Shaking his head, he chose a man and a woman from the hands raised.

Matt shot to his feet. "But—"

The hall door opened. An officer escorted a woman into the room. Nadia Parker.

****

Her protective officer by her side, Nadia approached

the high carved door to the conference room. She pressed a hand to her stomach, tied in granny and square and three other kinds of knots. She'd barely slept or eaten. Too difficult to get comfortable on a pillow wet with tears. And everything Officer Wade, her babysitter at the safe house, prepared, tasted bitter. Like regret.

How could she have fallen for his line *again*? Damn him and damn herself. And this time, she hadn't just lost her senses, she'd lost her heart. What was that saying—fool me once, fool me twice? She couldn't remember how the rest of that went. Enough, no more moping, wallowing in self-pity. At least until this mission, op, whatever the hell they called it, was over. She could hold off the bleakness until Sari was safe. She had to be tough.

"Here we are," the woman said. She'd insisted on her first name. Nadia felt like less of a prisoner calling her Vanessa. "It'll be fine. Officer Stratton has a few things to go over, and then I'll deliver you to Her Highness's apartment."

"Thanks, Vanessa, you've been very kind." She smoothed her damp palms down her tunic top. Someone from DARK had retrieved her suitcase from the Bethesda hotel and brought her the bill, which she refused to look at for now. Maybe she could pay the credit card a little at a time. That and disinterring her film company from the pit would have to wait. But wearing her own top and favorite black pants buoyed her confidence. She sucked in a breath as Wade opened the door.

The loud voices she'd detected through the closed door hushed as they entered. The artist part of her brain kicked in, perhaps to keep her sanity intact, and she endeavored to imagine the whole thing—the planning, the staging at the refugee center, Cardona's plot—as a documentary.

Men and women sat around a huge rectangular table, tablets notepads and coffee mugs scattered before them.

One person was standing. Matt Leoni.

Her knees wobbled, threatening to buckle. She swallowed and gripped the back of the empty chair before her. His gaze turned razor sharp and his features morphed into a stony mask. Still, she had no trouble detecting that shadows colored his eyes and deep lines bracketed his mouth. He looked every bit as haggard as she must. Good.

Or maybe he was preparing to go undercover. His scruff meant he hadn't shaved in at least three days. Damn him for making her want to run her hand over his jaw.

She forced her gaze to the officer who'd now come to his feet. It was Cole Stratton, a tall, rugged-looking officer who'd been introduced to her yesterday.

He smiled and gestured to the empty chairs, apparently saved for her and Vanessa. "Welcome to our meeting, Ms. Parker. Please have a seat."

Only then did she realize she had a white-knuckle grip on hers. She nearly fell into the chair. Vanessa took the adjacent one. Nadia breathed a sigh of relief that the woman had stayed. She wasn't alone. Unavoidable in her peripheral vision, Matt sat and cupped his hands around his coffee. Deliberately, she turned her attention to Stratton and wound her fingers together to prevent drumming on the table.

He said, "Everyone, this is Nadia Parker, who'll be central to our takedown of Sandor Cardona and his rebels. Ms. Parker, we're grateful to you for your courage in taking the role of Princess Sarika."

Mustering a smile, she swept the assemblage with her gaze, skimming past Matt.

They looked at her in somber silence, and a shudder worked through her. What must they be thinking? That in two days they would have to protect her from an assassination? Or that she looked too panicky to follow through and they'd have nothing?

"We all appreciate how stressful the situation is for you as a civilian," said Stratton.

"Yes," said one of the several women officers, "and we'll all be there primed to protect you."

Stratton took over. "We do have Her Highness on board, although she threatened World War III if anything happened to you." His comment elicited a few smiles and nods, but not from Nadia. And not from Matt. Stratton clicked something, and a slide appeared behind him, showing the area in front of the refugee center. He pointed out a few locations where officers would be stationed. Information she'd already examined.

Simon Byrne had showed her the slides yesterday. He and Thorne detailed the arrangements for the ribbon cutting. They didn't mention and she didn't ask if Matt would be one of the agents there. Did she want him there? He would do his best to protect her. She knew that. But—

"We've added an extra layer of protection. Two officers will be with you on the dais," Stratton said.

The man and woman who'd volunteered rose briefly.

Much better than being up there alone. The tension in her linked fingers eased. Oh, his questioning gaze meant she needed to respond. She squared her shoulders.

"I'm grateful for all the care you're all taking with this plan. I'll hold up my end. Do you know if Cardona will show?"

"We have intelligence that he'll be there, along with some of his men. We don't know who's expected to… attack. You'll wear a bulletproof vest and a transceiver. That's a miniature transmitter so we can communicate with you and you with us. Officer Wade will be in the command post, so if you spot Cardona, you can alert her."

Finally, the words "attack" and "bulletproof vest" canceled the tame scenarios she'd conjured when she'd entered this room. Not even a docu-drama about an assassination, this would be a thriller starring her as the target. And it, in DARK jargon, went down tomorrow afternoon.

Vanessa squeezed her hand, and she squeezed back, but couldn't manage a smile.

As Matt rose, he caught her attention. He bent over the table, splayed his hands on the surface and speared her with a dark, glittering gaze. "You don't have to go through with this, Nadia. You can end it right now. Say the word and we abort."

She drew a deep breath and lifted her chin. "No. I'm in. I need to do this."

Chapter Twenty-One

NADIA SIPPED THE excellent Frascati, a dry Italian white, Sari had said. More than a few sips might not be a bad idea, to black out the turmoil whirling a bruise-black tornado inside her.

The housekeeper had just set a silver tray with canapés and the drinks on the cocktail table. On her way out the door, she announced that dinner, ratatouille, was in the oven.

"Thank you, Bianca," Sarika called to her.

The woman wished them both a good evening.

Their damask-covered wing chairs huddled together in a sunlit corner of Sari's living room. The cushy earth-toned seats ought to soothe her fractured nerves, so why didn't they? Oh, yes, the cinnamon color reminded her of the taste of Matt's mouth on hers. Her stomach tightened, and she set down her wine. Dammit, when would the blasted man stop invading her thoughts?

"To answer your question, no, you can't talk me out of going through with my impersonation. But how did they persuade you to go along with my scheme?"

Her friend laughed, more of a half-hearted chuckle. "They didn't. Simon Byrne simply told me and asked if I'd lend you clothing. For what it's worth, I said you were bonkers and called the whole lot of them idiots."

High-handed jerks would be more accurate. Nadia nodded toward the bone-china tea service beside the wine bottle. "You're not joining me?"

Her friend shook her head, but winced at the movement. She looked her cool and elegant self in a violet silk top and purple designer jeans, despite bandages and a metal walker that waited beside her like a skinny-legged service dog. "Pain pills, antibiotics, so no alcohol." She stirred a spoonful of sugar into her teacup.

"You can't know how sorry I am this happened to you." Only yesterday had Nadia learned the exact nature of the wounds Sari suffered. Bruises everywhere. Deep lacerations on her legs and more cuts on her left arm. A concussion from the impact on the balcony's stone floor. "And poor Pascale…" Her voice faltered, but she forged on. "If I hadn't hired those men—"

"Rubbish! Not a blinking thing of it was your doing. Sandor Cardona would've found another way to attack me. A car bomb. A sniper. I'd have died, and you and Matt would not have been there to sort out the mess. So enough groveling. Stefan drove me to visit Pascale's family yesterday. I've arranged for them to accompany her casket home."

Nadia nodded, unable to express her regrets further. Under escort, she too had visited the family. She knew the royal family would provide more than transportation for the grieving one.

Her smile poignant, Sari lifted one shoulder in a shrug of dismissal. "And you moving my chair by the balcony window saved my life. The chair blocked most of the debris."

"That's what Matt said." Nadia heaved a sigh, remembering. Dammit.

"Something has happened between you and Matt,"

Sari said, one sculpted eyebrow raised. She held her cup and waited, the smile on her face indicating her satisfaction that she'd leaped into the opening Nadia provided by mentioning Matt.

Nadia's distress must show on her face. She'd never been able to hide her emotions from her friend. "Modena Security would've shot us. He saved my life. We were on the run for nearly three days. Isn't that enough?"

"Not half." Sari leaned forward. "We've known each other since we were children. What are you not telling me? You know I'll not stop."

Nadia curled her lips inward and stared at her empty hands. Why not? Perhaps she'd feel better after ripping out the aching stone that was her heart. Then she could focus on what she'd face tomorrow. "I don't want to ruin your friendship with Matt."

Sari's smile was indulgent as she lifted her teacup to her lips. "I can handle a few harsh truths, and he's a big boy."

Indeed he was. Nadia's face grew warm. She took a fortifying swallow of her wine. "Then I hope you're comfortable, because this will take a while. It began five years ago when DARK was investigating my father." She cradled the goblet in both hands and kept her gaze on the crimson contents as she related her sorry tale. Sari asked a few questions and murmured understanding or sympathy occasionally, but otherwise made no comments. Nadia finished with her discovery that he'd recorded her call to her dad. She looked up. "He *spied* on me. So you see why I can't trust him."

"I see why you were reluctant to become involved with him this time and why you're angry now. What I see in Matt is an honorable man whose agency is extremely important to him, and not merely as a job. He believes in the mission of DARK, in protecting this country."

"I know that. His colleagues are his friends, his family. His only family." Suddenly aware of how tightly she gripped the goblet, she set it down.

"I see you do know. So why then do you suppose he 'spied' on you, as you put it?"

Nadia's chest tightened. They'd worked together after fleeing the embassy, and he seemed to trust her, even left her alone to join him. Then at the hotel, he comforted her and they made love. She came up with only one reason for the spying. Even thinking that word now brought bile up her throat. "DARK ordered him to."

"Exactly. He argued that you were trustworthy, but in the end, complied. Tell me again what he did when the bomb exploded and Security fired on you."

Silence weighted the air between them.

Nadia met her regal gaze. "He got me out of the building and we fled."

Every inch her island country's trade negotiator, the princess held her head straighter. "And did he not then break every rule and every regulation—regs, as he would say—to go on the run with you, to protect you from Security and the FBI, from the rebels, from interrogation?"

"Yes, yes, yes, he did all that. He risked everything. But he lied to me about recording my call to Dad. He'd sworn he didn't come on to me to spy on me, and…" She couldn't continue without another drink of wine to cool her throat. As she swallowed, an incongruity niggled at her brain. "Sari, how do you know about Matt's orders and what happened?"

"From another rule breaker, of course." She waved away the protest on Nadia's face. "Why do you think Matt played the recording?"

Nadia didn't know the answer, so said nothing.

Sari sipped her tea and waited.

Nadia pressed the heels of her hands to her tired eyes and concentrated. DARK had ordered Matt to spy on her in spite of his protests. He knew from everything she'd done that she was trustworthy. But Ritter and some others did not. "To prove my honesty, my loyalty?"

"Spot on. This morning, he pushed for more protection for you. And didn't he also try to stop you from risking your life? He's hurting as much if not more than you are."

****

Matt stretched out at his desk, booted feet propped on an open drawer, head back on his laced fingers, eyelids half shut. He blew out a breath and rolled his shoulders, the muscles cramping from his show of relaxation. His arms ached with the urge to punch something.

Across the room, Cole Stratton conferred with Jackson Thorne and the other officer whose name escaped him about their roles tomorrow. They would stand a little behind Nadia on the dais, on either side, a prime vantage point for spotting trouble. Ready to hustle her away. They were already added to the official guest list as recent big donors the princess had invited. The set-up seemed workable.

And yet it could still all go to shit. If Nadia got… hurt, it would be Brussels all over again. His mind flashed on the mangled bodies of Nashota and Malik. He wouldn't let that happen to Nadia.

A few minutes later, the two officers filed out, Thorne sketching him a salute. Matt returned it. Stratton was keying in something, probably a report on the meeting.

Matt dropped his feet to the floor, rose, and crossed the room. "Thorne isn't the right guy for this, Cole."

Stratton stopped typing and folded his hands on the desk. "And you know this how?"

"He's too new. He doesn't know everybody. He might mistake one of ours for a goon. He hasn't been around long enough to be down with how we operate."

"Thorne's a professional, came to us from the U.S. Marshal Service. And he's up to speed. That it?" Stratton's expression said he knew it fucking wasn't *it*.

Matt clenched his fists behind his back. Going for nice and reasonable. "Look, you can still reconsider. Why not assign me to be on the dais with Nadia? She's angry with me, sure, but she knows damned well I'll protect her. She—"

"Nice try, but forget it. I got no worries about Thorne, and neither does the director. You, I'm not so sure about. And Nadia's lightyears more than angry. She would put a bullet in you herself if somebody gave her a gun."

Matt scrambled for more reasons, but Stratton held up a hand. "Give it up. I understand how you feel." He looked away for a moment, a muscle ticking in his jaw like he was remembering pain. "I was there once, a long time ago, only I was the one betrayed. Yeah, I know you're not at fault. You were doing your job."

"Hell, thanks for that anyway." He wasn't finished yet. He'd be there, watching, with the other officers, and he'd fucking take down Cardona or whoever his shooter was. He turned to go.

"In fact, it's probably better if you're not even at the ribbon cutting." Stratton's words spun Matt back around. "I'm assigning you to the team picking up Alina Greco."

Chapter Twenty-Two

NADIA TURNED HER head one way and then the other, studying the new her. Her hair was now the same golden-wheat shade and chignon style as Sarika's, and her face felt pampered with royalty-worthy lotions and cosmetics. She even smelled like a princess. In fact, she smelled like *this* princess. Grinning, she bent closer to the wall mirror. It didn't matter that her eyes weren't the same shade of green as her friend's, but her sleepless night had done some damage.

Not that looking tired would be a problem for her performance this afternoon. People would expect the princess to look wan and weak. She'd spent most of the night punching her pillow and rewinding their talk yesterday. Matt had given her no reason not to trust him, and when she heard her and her dad's voices on his phone, she reacted on instinct instead of using her brain.

Except for Matt being ordered to spy on her, she knew the rest—the need inside him to belong, the dedication to his work and his team, the risks he'd taken for her. He wanted her, but did he truly care for her? On her way to bed, Sari had bandied the L word, but *she* couldn't bring herself to think it. He couldn't deny recording the phone conversation for obvious reasons. He surely knew how she'd feel, so he stayed away. She pressed a hand to her roiling stomach.

Suffer? Maybe, but he did appear wrung out

yesterday. But why would he still care for her? He must think her a petty bitch. How could she make it right?

Sari appeared in the mirror beside her. "The color and style suit you."

Nadia pulled her thoughts and unraveled emotions back to the present. "It's incredible how much we resemble each other. More than I realized."

"Come with me," the princess said. "I have secrets to share."

"Secrets? What kind of secrets?"

But Sari had steered her walker out of the guest bathroom and was hobbling down the long hallway.

Nadia joined her in the kitchen, where mottled gold spilled through the skylight and on the café table and chairs. Sari had poured coffee for them. The rich aroma wove warmth around them.

"What's this about?" Nadia took the wrought-iron chair Sari had pulled close to hers. Scenarios reeled through her mind. Maybe it was about the plots against the Modena royals. But maybe more violent plots were being launched by the terrorists. Or was it a secret about Sarika herself?

"There's a good reason we strongly resemble each other. Now that your father has told you the truth about your birth, it's time you knew the full story." She stirred cream and sugar into the cup, slowly, as if searching for words in the milky mixture. "You and I are first cousins."

Nadia gaped. "Have you pole vaulted to this conclusion because of what I told you?"

"No pole vaulting. I might damage my stitches." When Nadia only stared at her, Sari took a sip of her coffee. "It's a long story. I learned about this only a couple of weeks ago, so I don't know everything."

Moisture sheened her eyes, and she set down her cup.

"What is it? Please tell me."

Sari reached across the small table, and Nadia grasped her hand. Finally she spoke, in a tremulous voice. "Your mother left Modena pregnant with you, as your father said. She'd had an affair with my uncle."

A riot of emotions twisted Nadia's lungs, so she could scarcely get her breath, but managed to rasp out, "Your uncle... not the *duke*?"

"Uncle Roman, yes." Sari's shoulders straightened, as she'd gained control of her emotions. "As a palace secretary, Irena was a frequent emissary between him and my parents. He could be very charming. He was about ten years older than her, so it's quite likely he seduced her, the randy old goat." She huffed.

Nadia had seen photos of the king's brother, a tall handsome man with a military posture. The duke... and her *mother*? But that would mean....

"She and my mother were friends before Father ascended to the crown. I had just been born a couple of months earlier," Sari continued. Her words seemed to run into each other, colliding in Nadia's head and racing heart.

Sari's mother had found Irena crying and dragged the story from her. Back then, her pregnancy would've been a major scandal in the royal family and in the country, so Sari's grandparents and parents—and the duke—kept the secret. Irena left for the United States with new clothes, a generous bank account, and the keys to an apartment in Arlington, Virginia, all paid for by the duke.

A cyclone roared and swirled in Nadia's head. "The apartment was next to Dad's. It's how they met. I never suspected any of it. Is there more?"

"Merely the best news. The tabloids will have a field day, but times have changed. You have always been the sister of my heart. And now *all* the Constantins will welcome you into the family." She opened her arms.

Sniffing back tears, Nadia scooted closer and circled her arms loosely around her. "I don't want to hurt you… your injuries."

The sun glistened on Sari's tears and her wide smile. "You cannot. It is my joy to share this with you."

"Oh, Sari." Nadia held her cousin—*my cousin*—and let the tears come. "My… mascara…"

"Hush, we can take care of the fallout from a few tears of joy."

A soft hopeful warmth suffused Nadia. A family, a very large family in Modena. But without her film project and, oh God, her company, she couldn't afford to go to Europe. What would she do? And her father, she had to tell him all this, didn't she? What would he think? She'd been advised not to contact him yet, and this time she would take that advice.

But dammit, what was she going to do? What would Matt say? Ah, Matt. She pictured his brown eyes, tortured with fear for her yesterday, but still sexy, his slow moves and quick mind and his broad shoulders. He'd protected her, and yet he made her feel she could face anything, do anything.

And she could. She was ready for this afternoon's scenario. *Yes, a scenario. Think about it as a script.*

****

With Wade and Chief Renzo of Modena Security, Matt stood to one side of Alina Greco's apartment door. Another DARK officer and two more Security people flattened themselves against the wall on the other side. In case Greco was armed or any of Cardona's rebels were camped out inside, all held sidearms and wore official ballistic vests.

Another Security guy out of uniform—tousled black hair, Hollywood smile—shifted from foot to foot in front of the door. He dressed the same as the searchers at the Prospect Hotel. Pressed jeans, crisp jacket, polished military shoes. Matt would check into him later.

The guy swiped his hands down the sides of his jacket. Gearing himself up.

Matt chafed at the wasted time. He checked his wristwatch. One fifteen. The ribbon cutting at the Capital Refugee Resettlement Center was to start at two. He'd need at least a half hour to get from here in Adams Morgan to northeast D.C. Maybe longer. Was Nadia already there on the little stage, with God knew how many people milling around?

He looked at his watch again. Fuck. *Get on with it.* He couldn't say it aloud. This was Renzo's show.

Throat clearing from the chief pressured the guy to ring the doorbell. The standard *ding-dong* sounded inside. He smiled in the direction of the peephole and waited. His hands again did the napkin thing on his jacket.

A minute later, high heels clicked on the foyer floor. "Bruno, what are you doing here?" Alina said in Italian. Her voice rang with impatience. Matt knew the emotion intimately.

"Ciao, Alina," Bruno said. "I heard you took the day. It's my day off too, so I thought we could do something."

Fucking lame, but maybe enough to get the door

open.

"You thought." Her tone implied that clearly he hadn't thought, or he wouldn't have showed up.

Renzo lifted his hands palms up, mutely conjuring what charm the other man might possess.

Bruno must've had good peripheral vision because sweat began to bead on his temple. "Ah, my apologies, Alina. I hoped we had a connection, that you feel as I do."

His sad puppy-dog eyes must've done the trick because locks began to click open.

The door swung inward and Alina appeared. "Of course I do," she said sweetly, "but you should've phoned first. I have to go ou—" Her gaze lit on movement or shapes beyond the opening, and she took a step back inside.

Before she could slam the door, officers grabbed her arms and had her against the corridor wall, her arms and legs spread. She was relieved of a small pistol concealed in her ankle boot. When she spotted Matt and Renzo, a torrent of Italian curses flew from her mouth.

Matt honored her with a little bow as he and Wade, pistols held in both hands, hurried into the apartment. Place smelled of fake apple scent from a room freshener. Open plan kitchen and sitting area. Phone on the eating bar beside a honkin' big purse. The two of them made a sweep of the bedrooms, closets, bath.

Wade stowed her pistol. "I'll wrap up the computer equipment in the second bedroom."

"Clear," Matt called to the others. "Nobody here."

Modena had the authority over its national, but the embassy contained no facilities for prisoners. The plan was for Alina to be taken to DARK headquarters, which housed interrogation rooms and a secure suite. Modena Security and DARK would question her, and she would remain locked up until the Modena authorities could arrange for her transportation home to stand trial.

One twenty-five. Shit. Matt had arranged with Wade and the other DARK officer that he could split once Alina was in custody and the apartment secured.

"Go." She brushed her hands at him in a shooing gesture. "Make sure your woman is safe."

Her bald statement hit him like a punch to the gut. Not likely Nadia would ever be his anything, but he had no time to disabuse Wade of the notion. He headed for the door. "Thanks. I owe you both."

Renzo stepped in front of him. "Officer Leoni, I must speak with you."

No getting past the brawny man without a forklift, and his gravelly voice made the request a command.

Matt summoned patience. "Chief, your people and the other DARK officers can handle the rest here. I'm needed elsewhere." In case the ambassador hadn't informed her security chief about the trap for Cardona, Matt said no more. He moved his shoulders in an elaborate shrug, a gesture the other man should understand implied confidentiality.

"I will take only a little moment. First I must apologize to you and to the so lovely *Signorina* Parker for my... mistrust and mistreatment of you. I believed you were the bombers, you see. I was angry that I had allowed you—the bombers, I mean—to escape. We traced the *signorina*'s phone, and you understand I wanted to redeem myself. Instead... by being captured, my man further embarrassed Modena Security." He placed his hand over his heart, and his cheeks reddened.

"I hope we can keep this little misadventure between us."

Matt glanced at his wrist. One thirty. Dammit, he had to get the fuck out of here. "I accept your apology. But it won't go so easy with DARK. My superior doesn't like unsolved mysteries. This one needs to be cleared up. Best if you do that yourself."

The security chief's complexion deepened to maroon, but then he nodded and stepped aside.

Matt ran out the door. He punched the elevator button. Why did Alina have to live on the tenth fucking floor? What was happening at the center? Were all the DARK people in place?

A groan rumbled through him, and he clicked the Off switch on his imagination. Otherwise he'd be no good to anybody, least of all Nadia. He called on the focused calm an op like this one required, and let it settle around him like a mantle.

As he was contemplating a dash down the stairs, the elevator doors whooshed open.

Two minutes later he raced away from the building on his motorcycle.

Chapter Twenty-Three

MATT LEFT HIS bike on a side street and trotted toward the refugee center. When he got close enough to see the gathering crowd, he tugged up his sweatshirt hood so it drooped over his forehead. The sun would cook him soon, but he couldn't take a chance on being recognized.

He was fucking late. The ceremony had already started. Somebody was speaking, man or woman, he couldn't tell which. He set the frequency on his transceiver and inserted it in his ear so he could hear the DARK officers' chatter. Freeing the strap on his belt holster, he slowed his pace and ambled into the audience.

Crowd amounted to about seventy-five people, but more were arriving. All around him people jostled and pressed toward the speaker. They aimed cameras and iPads above those in front of them. Closer to the dais, members of the press also held up recorders.

He located Nadia up there. Seated up front to the right of the speaker, head held high, she wore a shawl over one shoulder of a green dress. Damn, if she didn't look exactly like Sarika! He drew a deep breath to ease the tightness in his chest. The two DARK officers stood close behind her. In suits, they fit in with the rest of the dignitaries. Except for their gazes, not on the speaker but focused on tracking crowd movements.

He pictured Sandor Cardona's thick black hair and

narrow, wolfish face but saw nobody close to that description. Perhaps the coward sent only his minions and expected to get outta Dodge with Alina Greco.

No. Cardona was a hands-on asshole. He was here. Matt just had to find him.

He glanced upward behind the dais, to the window where Wade was manning the communications. Being in the crowd looking toward the stage with everybody else wouldn't allow him the best vantage point.

The speaker, some D.C. city official, finished her glowing tributes. Matt weaved through the people clapping and toward the right side of the gathering. He skirted the stragglers and made his way to the corner of the dais.

"Hold it right there. I don't see no fuckin' press pass on y'all."

Matt turned to face a linebacker in a D.C. Metro police uniform. The cop held a pistol on him.

****

Nadia peeled her fingers apart and smoothed the pashmina she'd worried into pleats. She folded her hands and forced herself to sit still. Sari wouldn't fidget. Sari would be calm and serene. The ruse would hold. People see what they expect to see. She hoped that semi-rule held sway today.

The dais, merely a wooden platform covered in a rubber mat, spread before the entrance to the Capital Refugee Resettlement Center. Walking in the hesitant pace befitting an invalid, she'd made her way up the two steps leaning on the metal cane that now lay at her feet. Not much of a weapon. Thank God she wasn't left unguarded. A man and woman sent by DARK had accompanied her. And now they had her back, literally.

Knowing they stood behind her, armed, wasn't enough to dull the spiked balls in her stomach.

She took a deep breath, not easily accomplished in the tight-fitting ballistic vest beneath her jacket. Squinting in the bright sun, she surveyed the crowd. People of all hues and shades, traditional clothing from Africa and South America and the Middle East, places ravaged by repression and conflict. She caught wisps of patchouli and jasmine.

Her thoughts drifted to camera placement and framing the faces. This event should've been a segment in her documentary, a tribute to Sari's generosity and kind spirit. Thanks to people like her, these men, women, and children would benefit from education and job training and housing through this new center. At least a dozen reporters and photographers, all wearing plastic press passes on their jackets, ranked in front of the dais. A blonde woman wrote furiously on a reporter's pad when she wasn't recording on her phone, a bald man held a camcorder to his face, and a man wearing a Sikh turban held up a digital recorder. People still arriving were swelling the number to what she judged was already a hundred.

Among all those, she couldn't find the one she ached to see. She'd spotted Simon Byrne. And others who stood out. They could be either refugees or other agency people—or even rebels biding their time. No Matt Leoni, and no one resembling Sandor Cardona either. The rebel leader must be here. Somewhere.

She peered over the heads of the crowd. A man in a gray hoodie slouched through the crowd, head covered and bent as if he didn't want to be identified. A shudder worked through her, and she pulled the pashmina higher on her shoulder. She'd worn it to conceal the bulky vest.

Applause jerked her back. The speaker had finished, and the refugee center's director was introducing her. No, was introducing *Princess Sarika of the Republic of Modena*.

Heart beating hard enough to crack a rib, Nadia gripped the cane and pushed to her feet. Her DARK escorts stood and pressed closer. She stepped to the mic.

She'd practiced the speech. Her accent was okay, checked by Sari. Although her voice pitch was a tone higher, if anyone in the crowd noticed, they'd put it down to weakness. She needed no reminder to sound fragile. This had to work. "Thank you to everyone for coming on this joyous occasion."

To her left, chairs scraped and a man shouted, "Wait! Stop her!"

That imperious voice. Dominic Traynor. He must've realized she wasn't the princess. He would ruin everything. Cardona would disappear. Sari and her family would remain in grave danger. Terrorists would continue funding the rebels.

"She's not—" Before Traynor could finish, the two officers guarding her tackled him to the floor and held him face down.

Nadia could barely suck in air past the stranglehold on her throat. She turned back to the mic.

The crowd waited, murmuring among themselves. People craned their necks trying to see what was happening on the dais. More commotion behind her suggested the officers were escorting Traynor off the dais and away. Chairs scraped and rattled as the dignitaries again took their seats. The center's director hovered near Nadia, her mouth tight, her gaze worried.

Nadia waved her away. She could breathe again, and maybe she could proceed. *Should* proceed. She was left unprotected, but…

She mentally shook herself and worked up a smile. "My apologies for that rude interruption." A thunk drew her gaze downward. The bald man had dropped his camcorder. "It has been my great honor to—"

She watched the bald man reach into his jacket pocket. He looked up at her, his eyes gray ice. She knew that narrow face and narrow nose. *Cardona.* He was raising a pistol.

She couldn't move. Her limbs were lead, her feet cemented to the floor.

"Nadia! Down! Get down! *Now!*"

The pop of gunfire shattered her inertia. *Matt.* She flung the metal cane at Cardona and dropped, flat, onto the rubber mat. Shrieks and shouts from everywhere. The pounding of people running.

Close by, a gunshot blasted her ears. A heavy body landed atop her at the same time as one more shot exploded.

Silence.

A low voice rumbled in her ear. "I… got him, honey. Are you… okay?" He rolled off her onto his back. The hood of his gray sweatshirt fell away. The smoke around them carried the pungent smell of gunpowder.

She twisted to a sitting position and reached for him. "Matt, how?"

His eyes were closed. He shook his head. On a gut-deep moan, he pressed both hands to his chest. Crimson stained his right sleeve and was spreading.

"*Help!* Help me! This man's been shot!"

****

183

Matt didn't make it back to DARK headquarters until Wednesday afternoon. Damn hospital. He'd been shot in the arm, not the chest. Docs and nurses deflected his protests with words like infection and loss of blood. Hell. Even worse, the only person who came to visit him was Ken Ritter, who shifted from foot to foot as if working up an apology. Never got there. Damned right. Matt didn't want to make nice with the man.

So here he sat going over everything with Stratton, Byrne, and the others. They talked about Nadia, who had looked so beautiful and pale with an invisible target on her chest. Braver than him, for damn sure. He pulled himself from maudlin thoughts and back to his report.

"I yelled a warning to Nadia as I ran out onto the platform. Cardona fired." He gestured at his arm, bandaged and in a sling. "I landed hard, lost my breath but fired back. Got him in the numbers as I covered Nadia. Arrogant bastard wore no vest. Or maybe he expected to die a martyr. A bullet—reflexive move as he fell—hit my arm.

"Whole thing was a clusterfuck," he continued. "Too many civilians around. We were damned lucky nobody got hurt. Nobody innocent."

"We didn't anticipate that big a crowd." Byrne scraped fingers through his shaggy hair. "The director told me he's had phone calls from Congress."

Matt wanted to say *I told you so*, but let it slide.

He'd failed to keep Sarika safe, but the docs said she'd heal completely, and he'd made it to Nadia in time to protect her. Maybe he could trust himself again. Or not. A little self-doubt would hone the edge on his alertness, wouldn't it?

The painkillers had worn off, and he wanted out of

here. Damn arm hurt like a bastard, more than movies would have you think bullet wounds did. He wrapped his chewing gum in its paper and tipped two of his prescription pills into his hand. He'd switch to ibuprofen once he got home.

Wade slid him a water bottle. He winked his thanks to her.

Sarika's office and everything in it had sustained too much damage to be certain, but everybody agreed it was likely the phony film-crew guys had concealed the bomb in one of their cases. The reason Kelmen was in such a sweat to get the interview over with. The two men expected to have time to exit the building and disappear before the explosion. Poor suckers. Leave no witnesses was Cardona's style. Alina's job was to make sure of that. She held her phone in her hand when she left Sarika's office and passed Nadia and him in the anteroom. While he was comforting Nadia, Alina had time to duck into an empty office or her own. She phoned whoever called Security and then triggered the bomb. Killing all the film crew would've left no suspects to question. Unlucky for her that he and Nadia didn't die.

Others added their reports. Officers had spotted three of Cardona's men during the gathering. Now in custody, the rebels were spilling everything. It might've been because somebody hinted that otherwise they'd be turned over to their buddies the terrorists. One led officers to Cardona's lair and his laptop, where they found proof of the deal with New Dawn and of the attempts on the royals. If more digging found a connection to the Kremlin, Matt wouldn't be surprised. They also had proof for Modena officials of Alina Greco's tie to the rebel leader, but nothing indicated that her boss, Minister Ingel, was involved or even suspected her. When her involvement was revealed, he'd turned as pale as snow and nearly toppled over. The rest of the rebel bunch in the country had been identified and would be scooped up at the border or an airport.

Dominic Traynor was really in love with Sarika and had worried about why somebody was impersonating her, but he also was spying for the prime minister, his reason for skulking around the embassy.

The monarchy and parliamentary democracy in Modena were saved. If only the rescue and clearing up who did what would also result in saving Nadia's future with her film company.

When the meeting mercifully came to an end, Stratton took Matt aside. "Hey, man, the wrap-up of yesterday's fun and games ran long, but I finally collected your bike. Sweet ride. It's parked in your building's garage." He handed over the keys.

"Appreciate it, Cole. No riding for me for a while." He pocketed the keys.

"Won't be long. Go home. Get some rest." Stratton walked away talking on his phone.

Chapter Twenty-Four

MATT EDGED AWAY from the DARK employees spilling out onto the sidewalk and headed home. He was searching his phone for the ride-hailing app when he spotted Sarika's chauffeur heading toward him. The black limo stood at the curb.

"Hey, Stefan, what's up?"

The older man bobbed his head in a small bow. "Her Highness thought you might appreciate a ride home. At your service, sir." He doffed his chauffeur cap and held it chest high. Tears glittered in his pale blue eyes. "For myself, I thank you for what you did for my princess and my country."

Matt's gut tightened and his jaw clenched. *Just doing my duty* wouldn't cut it. He clasped the old man's hand. "Stefan, your princess is my friend. Although I failed to keep her safe, everything turned out okay in the end. Taking down that son of a bitch Cardona and the other traitors was a damned great pleasure. Lead me to that limo."

Stefan's grin fanned wrinkles across his entire face. He hustled ahead and opened the door.

The first thing Matt saw as he climbed inside was a strappy red shoe tapping on the plush carpet. The high heel was attached to a sexy foot and a dynamite female leg in a short black skirt. The rest of her lay in shadows. *Nadia.* His chest tightened as if a fist had squeezed the bruises from the inside.

As he slid into the seat beside her, he inhaled the scent of lilacs.

Her slender throat moved as she swallowed, and her soft gaze lowered to her hands.

He caught his reflection in the security window. No wonder she'd looked away from his dead-eyed glare, harsher than the G-man mask she'd accused him of wearing. But tension had him in its grip. He couldn't relax until he knew what she wanted.

He seemed to have come out of the hospital with a limited vocabulary because the same question he'd asked Stefan popped from his mouth. "What's up?"

She lifted her chin and faced him. Tangled emotions guttered behind her eyes. "How's your arm?"

He'd shrug, but the movement would dial up the pain in his arm. "I'll live."

Why was she in Sarika's limo? To say goodbye? Didn't she already do that? He didn't need a second thrashing and couldn't bear chitchat, not with this woman who made him feel more than, hell, just *more*. He reached for the door handle, but Stefan was pulling away from the curb. "Nadia—"

"Let me, please." She pressed an index finger to his lips and yanked it away so fast, he might've imagined she'd touched him. "You took a bullet for me on Tuesday. You saved my life. For that, I'm deeply grateful."

"I think we're even. You were braver than me, taking such a huge risk. Staked out like a damn sacrifice." Thank God he'd gotten to her in time. He'd have lost and the world would've lost this talented and loyal woman who defended her traitor father no matter what and who would've laid down her life for her friend. His pulse revved into a higher gear.

The luxury car cocooned them in its plush upholstery and sound baffles, so he hardly knew they were moving. They could be anywhere. The world shrank to only the two of them.

Without thinking, he reached for her.

She held up a hand and scooted a few inches away on the seat. Steely resolve hardened her gaze. "I have more I need to say."

She wasn't finished? Now was when she'd tell him she never wanted to see him again, that a couple of days together was great, but sayonara. He shouldn't have gotten in the car. How much longer before they reached his condo building? Maybe he'd get out at the next red light. He bent his head and rubbed his nape.

"Years ago," she said, "I jumped to conclusions about you. I was wrong then, and I was wrong this time."

His head came up, and he watched her search for words. He'd never known Nadia to be at a loss.

"Matt, while we were on the run, I came to realize you hadn't used me and that you did have feelings for me. Afterward, when I heard my voice on that recording, my blood froze." She shook her head. A small smile plucked at one side of her mouth. "I know, the saying is about blood boiling, but the shock turned me cold. I didn't stop to think why you'd recorded my call or why you were playing it for Ritter. I just blew." She twisted her fingers together in her lap.

He'd fucking deceived her, kept information from her, spied on her, and she was *apologizing*? The fist clamping his chest eased. Maybe he'd have a chance to make things right, a chance with her. Damn, did he *ever* want to pull her into his arms. "I *did* spy on you. You don't have to—"

"Will you please stop interrupting me while I'm groveling!" Brow crimped, she tossed back her hair. When he held up his palms, she continued. "Without, um, pressure, I'd have eventually come to my senses, but by then it would've been too late for me to do anything about... *us*. Sari made me ask myself the tough questions, and now I know why she's such a tough trade negotiator. DARK didn't trust me and ordered you to spy on me. I get that now."

"I was following orders, and I confess I did more than record that call. Doing what I had to do ripped me apart."

"I know. I understand. Now." She touched a finger to his hand where it had a death grip on his knee and then placed her hand on his. Her palm was cool and comforting. "You recorded my conversation with Dad because it was your duty. You played it for Ritter because it proved my innocence."

He turned over his hand and curled his fingers around hers. If it was possible, he'd never let go. "So he would back off. I couldn't stand the thought of him interrogating you again. He didn't hear the rest, about your mom being pregnant." Director Nolan had listened to the entire conversation, but he'd get to the result of that.

"I appreciate it, but now it doesn't matter. I'll explain later. About your work and DARK, I understand how important all that is to you. When we were together, I watched you and paid attention to what you weren't saying. A habit or a quirk of my profession, I suppose. Since losing your parents, you've been looking for someplace to belong, someone to belong *to*, and DARK has become that. The mission is important to you, as are your colleagues." She tilted her head and waited.

Stratton, Byrne, Wade, Thorne, and the others were there for him as he was for them, on ops, in missions, but they were only a substitute, and now he knew what he really wanted. "You've brought it up before, but it took a while to sink in. I never thought of it that way, but wanting to belong feels right."

Before he could broach what he wanted now, beyond work, she went on. "I saw you slinking around yesterday in that gray hoodie, but I didn't recognize you. How did you know to rescue me?"

Grinning, he rubbed his nape. She didn't need to hear about his race from one side of the District to the other. Or about the cop who stopped him. Fast talking and flashing his DARK creds put the guy on Matt's side.

"I happened to be standing to the right of the dais. I didn't spot Cardona, but I saw the pistol."

"The shaved head was a good disguise. I didn't know him, and he was right in front of me. When he dropped the camcorder, I recognized his eyes, his narrow features. He... that gun." A shudder quaked her shoulders. "I froze, but then I heard your voice."

Cardona was raising the gun to shoot her. It had all happened in a flash, but it seemed like slo-mo. "I was afraid to fire with you standing there. So I yelled as I ran to you." That was when the bastard shot him. "I sweated it, hoping you remembered the last time. That second or two lasted an eon."

"I remembered. I dropped." Her smile was soft, plumping her delicious lips. "I remember everything, every moment from our stolen time together."

He took that as an invitation. He cupped her head and tugged her closer. She tilted against him and closed her eyes. When he dabbed both corners of her mouth with his tongue, she opened to him. His lips found hers, and they kissed with heat and hunger. Their tongues tangled, and she laid her hands on his shoulders and scooted closer so their hips touched. The open-mouthed kiss made his breath catch. He kissed her deeply, plunging his tongue into her sweet mouth, in imitation of what he longed to do with her again. In two seconds, his body went from interested to full-on desperation. He started to lift her onto his lap when a shaft of pain tore into his upper arm. He gasped for breath.

"Damn, damn, damn, your arm." Nadia held her hands away from him as if she'd been the fucking idiot who'd tried to lift her.

He grimaced. "I'm okay. If I had two good arms, we might've given old Stefan a shock when we arrived at my building."

"Only you could make a joke about your injury."

He slapped a hand on his chest. "Aargh, you wound me."

She rolled her eyes. "You rest. I have more to share. I know about my parentage. Sari told me."

"Sarika?" The knives stabbing his arm had subsided, so he settled again, riveted as she told him about an affair between her mother and her birth father the duke, both now gone. "Dad—he'll always be my dad—fell in love with Mom pretty much at first sight. He was so willing to marry a woman carrying another man's baby because he was sterile. It was his only chance for a family. I'd always wondered why I never had brothers and sisters."

"They loved each other?"

She nodded. "Mom loved him right back. When she was about to marry him, she called the queen and told her she wanted nothing more from the duke, that he was never to contact her—or me. Until then, he'd supported her financially. Sari said her mother always admired Mom for that. Now that the duke is dead, the family thought I should know."

"An amazing story." He straightened. "So Sarika is your cousin. Even more amazing. You look so much alike, so maybe not."

She lifted a lock of her hair. "I'm thinking of keeping this lighter color. Prettier than my dishwater blonde."

"I like it for Sarika, but it's not you. Your color's not dishwater, but dark honey." He smoothed his free hand over her hair, and she tilted her head into his touch, like a puppy being petted.

"Really? You like my real color?" A laugh punctuated her skepticism. "Very diplomatic, sir."

"Nobody'd ever mistake me for a diplomat, but I prefer the dark honey." He pulled her close and brushed her mouth with a kiss. "So you have relatives. Sarika's parents, the king and queen of Modena, are your aunt and uncle. That must've blown your mind."

"Once it sank in. And there's more. My mother's parents disowned her back then. But now that they've learned it was the duke who got her pregnant, they want to meet their granddaughter. I think association with the royal family might have something to do with their interest." She grinned. "Apparently I have an older half-sister and brother and a few nieces and nephews."

"I'm happy for you." He was, of course he was, but her good news had struck a nerve like a hammer blow.

He used to dwell on the loss of his parents—dark, savage brooding spells that he'd had to overcome or they would've owned him. If anybody deserved this happiness, it was Nadia. He banished his bout of petty envy. Needing to touch her again, he captured her hand and held on. "You have family now, more than you could've imagined. "Does your dad know?"

"Yes, and he thinks it's great." Her joyous smile turned downward. "He's being moved to the Federal Medical Center in Devens, Massachusetts, where they can treat him for the prostate cancer. You wouldn't know anything about that, would you?" She cocked her head and pursed her lips.

"Director Nolan pulled some strings, a sort of apology. The men who jumped your dad are being charged with aggravated assault and attempted murder. They're in a more secure section of the prison." He doubted whether DARK or any other agency would get from them who'd paid them. If they squealed, they'd be next for the hit squad.

"Good. They deserve whatever punishment they get. It'll be easier to visit Dad in the new place instead of out in the Pennsylvania boonies. They're moving him in a couple of days, and I'll go see him. The insurance company is coming through for me on the loss of equipment, and King Bernard wants me to continue the documentary. I'll finally do my interview with Sari. My usual crew are healed and will join me."

"Sure you don't need an inexperienced production assistant? Something I can do one handed?"

"For the interview, no. I'm told you're supposed to rest. You'll need to heal for the trip to Modena next month. The king wants to pin medals on us."

He gaped at her. "*Us*? You're joking."

"Nope. Without us, the rebels would've killed Sari and created more chaos. You're the one who told me I saved her from the bomb by moving her to the bay window. The whole sequence after that led us to Tiana finding Cardona's passport photo and me recognizing him as the man who met Alina." She frowned. "I wonder how she became involved with him and the rebels."

He huffed. "Ambition, maybe love. During questioning, she revealed he promised she'd play a big role once he took over the government."

"Must've been Ken Ritter who grilled her."

He made sure his expression was blank before he spoke. "I wasn't there."

"I see. Top secret." She wagged her shoulders. "Will DARK let you come to Modena with me? And what about repercussions from not following orders?"

"To answer the first, I'm due a bunch of vacation time, so maybe. As for the other, only a reprimand, mostly because everything turned out okay."

"Just okay?" Her throat worked as she swallowed. She cast a glance down at their joined hands and then watched him intently for a moment. "Didn't we find something in each other, something we both need? Belonging. And love?"

The iron-tight knot that had tied itself in his chest ever since he entered the car frayed apart and dissolved. Deep inside, an expansive feeling bloomed. His heart clanged cymbals and his soul soared. He squeezed her hand. It was all he could manage until he could speak.

"Nadia, I think I've been in love with you for five years, but I couldn't let myself think it. You're smart and caring and loyal and beautiful, and somehow you've found the places inside I never let anybody touch before. I kept telling myself I would never give up control of my life for anybody, but you helped me understand that belonging to—and with—somebody I love doesn't mean losing control. Except in bed."

She laughed, and he released her hand. He swept his thumb across her lower lip before he kissed her. She looped her arms around his neck and hung on for the ride.

When he ended the kiss, she started to speak, but he touched two fingers to her mouth. "Honey, it's complicated. *We're* complicated. My vision's improving every day, and I'll be back to field duty when the arm's better. You travel as much as I do, and you're out of the country more than in."

She kissed his fingers and smiled. "We'll find a way. If we want it enough, we'll make it work."

"We'll make it work."

Through the tinted side window, he recognized the statue at the entrance to the small park. Only a few blocks until they reached his building. "You coming with me to my place?"

"I am. I packed my suitcase."

"I'm wounded, you know."

"In the line of duty. My wounded warrior."

He held his injured arm and moaned. "Hurts like hell. I need TLC."

Her sultry smile made him want to rip off her clothes. "I know just what to do."

A word about the author...

Occasional bouts of insomnia led to Susan Vaughan's writing career. When she couldn't sleep, she made up stories to fill the long, dark nights. Her stories throw the hero and heroine together under extraordinary circumstances and pit them against a clever villain. Besides curling up with a good mystery or romance, Susan enjoys walking her dog, boating, traveling, and volunteering. A former teacher, she is a West Virginia native, but she and her husband have lived in Maine for many years. Susan is the author of 16 novels and one children's book. Find her at www.susanvaughan.com or at https://www.facebook.com/susanvaughanbooks.

Thank you for purchasing
this publication of The Wild Rose Press, Inc.

For questions or more information
contact us at
info@thewildrosepress.com.

The Wild Rose Press, Inc.
www.thewildrosepress.com